PUBLIC OFFERINGS

Book One

Birthright

A novel by

Bob LiVolsi

DEDICATION

To Susan who has patiently believed in me and encouraged me for far too long for her own good. Thank you, my darling wife, for being there always and for loving me. I love you always.

To all the people in generous communities of caring around the world who continue to sacrifice their comfort and often risk their lives to bring hope to our peers in less fortunate corners of the world. And to the people of Sierra Leone whose misery at the hands of warlords and power brokers informed the very first draft of this book all those years ago in 1995. Even at this writing, the struggles of the Leoneans and other West Africans continue as they deal with the largest Ebola outbreak yet recorded.

To all those who cling to and proclaim a faith of compassion for human beings, built on service not conquest, built on hope not rules, and encompassed by love — at all times recognizing a much greater force that transcends our personal demands and yet embraces our free will and individuality.

TABLE OF CONTENTS

EPIGRAPH   3

November 22

   PROLOGUE - Cameron Pass, Colorado   5

BOOK ONE – Birthright

October 14, Five Weeks Earlier

   CHAPTER 1 - Fort Collins, CO, Clement Home   7

   CHAPTER 2 - Lagos, Nigeria   10

   CHAPTER 3 - Clement Home   17

October 15

   CHAPTER 4 - Lagos, Nigeria   18

   CHAPTER 5 - Lokoma Village, Sierra Leone   23

   CHAPTER 6 - Clement Home   30

October 16

   CHAPTER 7 - Lagos, Nigeria   31

   CHAPTER 8 - Lokoma Village   32

   CHAPTER 9 - Liv's Diary   39

   CHAPTER 10 – Boulder, Colorado: Health Club   41

   CHAPTER 11 - Aldrich Institute HQs, Boulder   42

   CHAPTER 12 - Freetown, Sierra Leone   45

   CHAPTER 13 - Aldrich Lab, Cameron Pass   47

October 17

   CHAPTER 14 - Liv's Diary   50

   CHAPTER 15 - Lokoma Village   51

October 18

   CHAPTER 16 - Dave Clement's Office, Loveland   54

CHAPTER 17 – Freetown Peninsula, Lokoma Road   61

CHAPTER 18 – Freetown Peninsula, Lokoma Road   67

October 19

CHAPTER 19 - Aldrich Mountain Lab   69

October 20

CHAPTER 20 - Poudre River Canyon   73

October 21

CHAPTER 21 - Clement Home   79

CHAPTER 22 - Dave's Office   85

CHAPTER 23 - Aldrich HQs, Boulder   88

CHAPTER 24 - Fort Collins High School Gym   90

CHAPTER 25 - Dave's Office   92

CHAPTER 26 - Fort Collins High School Gym   95

CHAPTER 27 – Charco Broiler Restaurant, Fort Collins   98

CHAPTER 28 - Clement Home   103

October 22

CHAPTER 29 - 36,000 Feet above the North Atlantic   105

CHAPTER 30 - Clement Home   108

CHAPTER 31 - Aldrich Mountain Lab   109

About the Author   Appendix.... Page 2

Character Summaries   Appendix.... Page 3

PUBLIC OFFERINGS

BOOK ONE

Birthright

EPIGRAPH

When they came to the place that God had shown him, Abraham built an altar there and laid the wood in order. He bound his son Isaac and laid him on the altar, on top of the wood. Then Abraham reached out his hand and took the knife to kill his son.

But the angel of the Lord called to him from heaven and said, "Abraham! Abraham!...Do not lay your hand on the boy or do anything to him; for now I know that you fear God, since you have not withheld your son, your only son, from me."

Genesis 22: 9-1

PROLOGUE

Cameron Pass: Rawah Wilderness of northern Colorado,
Aldrich Mountain Lab
November 22, 11:10 p.m. Mountain Standard Time (MST)

In the thin air of Cameron Pass, where the peaks of the Colorado Rockies first scrape Wyoming sky, Sheila Stratemeier struggled late into the night with information she did not fully understand. Information about death. A lot of death. Avoidable death.

Her lab coat thrown over her cubicle wall, Sheila propelled her thin fingers in a manic jig across the keyboard. The phosphorescent blue light of the PC's display revealed squinting eyes and lips squeezed together over grinding teeth. The ethereal glimmer stood a beacon amidst a sea of cubicles in Dilbertville, a ghost town awaiting the arrival of the morning shift in just a few hours. The gloomy expanse echoed with the creaking and popping of metal vents, the vague howl of the mountain wind in counterpoint – each new variation causing Sheila to flash her eyes for a nervous glance along the battlements of her cubicle fortress.

She had nearly escaped. At 6:30, she started to leave the building for the lab's dorms, but the chill of autumn wind rushing across the compound gave her pause at the exit. The wrestling match in her conscience drove her back inside.

As senior research scientist for drug discovery at the Aldrich Institute, she had come to know many AIDS victims in the course of her research. She knew through first-hand observation the horrible, devastating, wasting death that often resulted. Any hope mattered.

But not this.

The project – this apocalypse – had to be stopped. Sheila did not know where to turn.

She held a sheet of paper up in the reflected light of the LED monitor. A long sigh. She dropped back in her chair, hands flung to her lap. After a moment, she raised her hands, held them poised over the keyboard.

A thud. She looked up. Waited. Quiet.

Her fingers dropped to the keyboard, pouring a flow of words across the screen. She would e-mail this document to the board of the Aldrich Institute before sunrise. She pondered sending a copy to Dave Clement, but decided, for the sake of his fifteen year old daughter, not to add to his burden. Not yet anyway.

If the Aldrich board failed to respond, she would feel justified in going to the press. That would also be the appropriate time to bring Dave fully into the loop. She already had gone so far as to load the phone numbers of the Denver Post and the mile-high city's Fox TV affiliate as favorites on her cell phone – which had no signal at the lab. Security.

She did not really want to involve the press. She did not want the headlines for herself or the lab. Bad press would undermine the great good the lab could do. Plus she would end up blackballed for life and probably cause Claire McQuaid and the Aldrich Institute to fight her all the harder. So she preferred to work through internal channels. No outsiders. No headlines.

The dance of her fingers accelerated on the keys, the flow of words streaming across the screen. The plastic bridge of her glasses slipped down her nose. A finger popped off the keyboard to push them back up.

Another thud. Nearby. She paused, scanned the top of her cubicle walls. Quiet.

Fingers poised again. Face back in the blue light.

A knock. She half rose from her seat, hovering, listening. A loud clatter. She stood, grabbed the top of the cubicle and peered over.

Her shoulders relaxed. She tapped on the top of the cube. Waved. Several cubicles away, a man wearing a gray institutional shirt waved back. He dumped a plastic trash can into a larger container. Sheila blew out, sat, fingers back on the keyboard.

The incessant rhythm of the clicking keys slowed only slightly when she sensed the movement behind her. She felt no pain when the wire sliced through her windpipe. When her body jerked from its chair, the garrote caught in the parts of her neck. Her hand reached out to hit the send key, barely missing. Airborne, she vaguely registered her loafers dangling off the toes of her naked feet. Her toes curled, trying to save the shoes. New shoes. An instant later, her air-starved nerves imploded, one final burst of confused data firing across screaming synapses.

In the end, Sheila made headlines after all.

CHAPTER 1

Fort Collins, Colorado – 64 Miles East of Cameron Pass,
Clement Home
October 14, 7:40 p.m. Mountain Time (MT)

FIVE WEEKS EARLIER…

Liv Clement did not want to be alone, especially not with a death sentence hanging over her head. The new meds should have helped but they only seemed to make her feel a little off center, a little disconnected from life. They definitely kept her up at night.

Per her doctor's orders, she downed an Ambien with a cup of water. She estimated she had forty-five minutes to an hour before she nodded off - if all went well.

She peered out the window to make certain her mom's car pulled away into the night. Below in the darkness, she watched the family's black SUV pull out of the garage, crunching over the fresh early season snowpack.

She tapped out a text on her phone.

Gone to her prayer group

A zipping sound pffted from the phone's speaker, marking the text's departure.

She crawled into bed as instructed by her mother, but she pulled out her phone and started texting again – in contradiction to her mother's instructions. With Dad tossed out of the house - and now away in Sierra Leone or Nigeria - she thought her Mom had become way overprotective. With her HIV diagnosis, Liv thought it only made sense to have more fun while she could, not freak out like her Mom. Plus, at fifteen years of age, she was old enough to be in charge of her own life.

Within 30 seconds, another pfft indicated a response from her best friend Chelsea.

Can you get out?

Liv replied.

Come over here.

Can't. Homework. But you can come help.

My mom would kill me. Tell your parents

you're coming here to do homework.

She chose not to tell Chelsea that she had to stay home because she had taken an Ambien. It would lead to other questions she did not want to answer. She waited for the next response. She laid her head on her pillow, looking up at the dark ceiling, marked by glow-in-the-dark stars. Tonight for some reason, they seemed to collide into each other, as though the ceiling were alive. She felt woozy and blinked to make the stars stop moving.

Chelsea's response did not come quickly. Checking with her parents, thought Liv. She looked at the time on her phone. Eighteen minutes since the sleeping pill. If Chelsea waited any longer it would be pointless.

Pfft. The response.

But another text showed on her screen. From someone else.

I see you.

She looked to see who the text came from. She did not recognize the phone number. She tapped.

Who is this?

The best thing that ever happened to you.

The phone number had a 720 prefix, meaning this intruder came from outside the Fort Collins 970 area code. Probably an automated program. Liv had heard of these. She had read that she should outsmart it with a question that required judgment and could not easily be anticipated by a software algorithm.

What am I wearing?

A pink half t-shirt. And tiny green silk underpants.

A bullet of fear shot through Liv. She grabbed her robe off the floor, threw it on and jumped out of bed to look out the window. She was on the second story and there were only snow-covered trees with bare limbs across the street. She jerked around. Her bedroom door was closed. She looked at her closet door. Closed, but it had louvered slats someone could look through. Slowly, she cracked the closet door to peek inside. Movement, A shadow.

She ran from the room, pressing 911 on her phone. Then the signal dropped.

"No. No. No!"

She ran down the stairs. In the kitchen, she grabbed the house phone. No dial tone!

She raced to the hall closet, slipping on the tile in her bare feet. Bouncing off one knee in the dark, she grabbed a coat and her snow boots. She flew through the front door and out into the snow barefoot, the boots and coat still in her hands. Suddenly, light flooded the yard. She stumbled back, falling into a drift. Every light in the house seemed to shine through the windows. The front flood lights cast long shadows of de-nuded Aspen trees, their spindly branches reaching like claws across the snow.

Liv screamed.

CHAPTER 2

Lagos, Nigeria – 6,890 miles east of Fort Collins
October 15, 6:37 a.m. West Africa Time (WAT)

Dave Clement absorbed the text from his wife. He felt his stomach tighten, anxiety taking firm hold.

> Came home to a mess. Liv hallucinating
> again. Pretty bad this time.

Mel didn't want him. But maybe she needed him. He wanted desperately to help Liv. He thought about her almost every moment of every day. He even risked his career to contact Sheila at the Aldrich for help. Yet Mel remained determined to keep him away.

He sat back in the polished mahogany pew and typed out a short question in reply.

> She ok?

> Yes. Finally fell asleep.

He looked at his watch. 6:37 in the morning in Lagos. That made it 10:37 the night before back in Fort Collins.

> What happened?

> I was at the grocery. Ludwins heard her
> screaming and took her in until I got
> home.

The Ludwins, the Clements' next door neighbors, did not like to deal with neighbors as friends, but they proved good in emergencies. Dave tapped again.

> What did she see?

> Thought a stalker texted her. Nothing
> on her phone.

> Stop the Ambien, Mel.

Doc Resnick has prescribed the sleep drug to help Liv deal with the insomnia caused by her meds and her anxiety. The doc considered using Xanax but in consulting with Dr. Ellis, the infectious disease specialist, he learned there was evidence it interacted with Liv's anti-retroviral, AZT, to actually cause insomnia. Dave thought Liv should take only the anti-retrovirals and see if the sleep issues worked themselves out. Mel disagreed. He waited for Mel's reply, hoping she would finally side with him against Doc Resnick's prescription pad. When she did not respond for several minutes, he knew he had irritated her.

He tapped in something more neutral to elicit response.

> Are you sure it's hallucinations? Maybe you should have the police look into it.

As soon as he hit "send", he realized he made a mistake. Mel did not like him telling her what to do, especially since the split. He traveled and worked so much that he rarely spent time with Liv. She had made it more than clear that she did not think he had the right or the knowledge to interfere with her decisions for their daughter, even when it came to pharmaceuticals - which was his profession.

Not surprisingly, Mel still did not respond. He thought about calling her, but knew they would likely end up in a heated discussion that would only keep her up all night and get his day off to a bad start.

So there he sat, feeling helpless and maybe just a little irresponsible in an empty church almost 7,000 miles away from home. He put the phone down on the pew and knelt on the kneeler. He had a lot to pray about.

He pulled a rosary out of his shirt pocket and wrapped it around one hand. Dusty rainbow-colored rays of sunrise passing through the stained glass shimmered kaleidoscopically off the tiny silver cross dangling at the end of the rosary's slender chain. He rolled the first tiny brown bead between thumb and forefinger and began to pray. "Our Father, Who art in heaven, hallowed be thy name. Thy kingdom come, Thy will be done on earth as it is in heaven…"

He found himself at the end of the prayer and on to a Glory Be before he realized that he had completely zoned out the words in the last half, the whole "Give us this day our daily bread" thing. He had thought the words on one track of his brain, but his focus had shifted somewhere else entirely. He pushed back the heartache, the hole in his stomach, the need for a rewind button for life.

He heard another text arrive. He snatched his phone off the pew, hoping for something conciliatory from Mel. Instead, this one came from Jennifer Winter, his project manager at the company's headquarters in Loveland, Colorado. A protégé of Claire McQuaid, Jennifer started her career working for Claire at the Aldrich before joining Dave's team at Prodeus where she managed the Portable DNA Analyzer (PDNA) program.

> Thinking of you. Hope the trip's going well.

"What are you doing, Jenn?" he mumbled out loud. Her thoughtfulness had little to do with their business relationship, particularly since it was almost 11 p.m. in Colorado and Jenn was probably lying in bed. She flirted with Dave constantly – or at least he thought she did - making him very uneasy. She seemed determined to drive the wedge in deeper between him and Mel, a problem he did not want. He ignored the text and returned to his prayers. He wanted God to fix Liv and fix his marriage. He wanted God to help Sheila Stratemeier come through with new and better drugs for Liv. But distractions kept racing through his mind. He tried to mumble the rote prayers out loud, to move his lips like the nuns and the priests taught him not to do. If he stayed focused, answers might come.

"Hail Mary, full of grace, the Lord is with thee. Blessed art thou among women and blessed is the fruit of thy womb..."

Even as he mumbled his prayers, his thoughts bounced around like a silver ball in a pinball machine, caroming off the bumpers that threatened the touchstones of his life. He envisioned Liv huddled in her bedroom, the drugs toying with her sanity, the source of her disease still a mystery while his inability to fix her tormented him. He re-lived Mel's iciness the night he came home to find himself locked out, his suitcase on the front porch, Mel insisting that he was hurting Liv and their family. He recalled his uneasiness and unwelcome sense of attraction as Jennifer violated his personal space at the office, leaning close enough to afford an unavoidable glimpse into her soft cleavage, her perfume thick and her breath warm. And Claire McQuaid's suffocating apparition seemed to occupy the pew with him, her relentless - and almost inexplicable - zeal demanding his full attention. Each phrase of his prayers seemed to be punctuated, like subtitles in a movie, by one of the project steps needed to meet Claire's aggressive Thanksgiving deadline.

Soon, the relentless staccato firing of his thoughts left him twenty Hail Mary's into his rosary, not remembering a word he mumbled. He held a single rosary bead tightly between his right index finger and thumb. He wanted desperately to concentrate on his prayers. "Hail Mary, full of Grace, the Lord is with thee. Blessed art thou among women and blessed is..."

His backyard came into his mind's eye. Something shook the branches on the Aspen trees along the back fence. Movement in the shadows. Liv's stalker. What if she was not hallucinating? He wanted desperately to be back in Fort Collins to protect her. He felt caught in the middle. He needed the money more than ever, the big pay day that would come with an initial public offering of the company's stock. That money would allow him to pay for experimental therapies - not covered by health insurance - giving him a chance to commute Liv's life sentence with HIV. Liv's disease had already developed resistance to the first round of medications. What if she built resistance to all the covered meds? That did not bode well. Experimental meds might ultimately prove to be her only viable option. He had already risked the ire of Claire McQuaid by secretly seeking advice from Sheila Stratemeier, the lead drug developer at the Aldrich. He had her swear not to share Liv's secret with others. She said she had some ideas she would research, but she told him any option would be very expensive. That meant Dave had no choice but to make the big bucks; he had to travel, had to stay on his toes almost 24 x 7 with the business, bound to be distracted instead of paying attention to the family details on the home front. And that destined him to piss off Mel. She claimed he used the job as an excuse for his work obsession. "It's just your nature," she accused. "It's not the job."

Finally, he put the rosary beads down. No use today, he thought. He needed medication to focus his mind. But he wouldn't take it. He never did.

His eyes moved to the main altar, to the image of Mary holding the baby Jesus patiently formed in the stained glass behind the altar. He grabbed the rosary again. His fingers passed through five beads of Hail Marys while he pondered the statuary. Without noticing, he had mumbled every word of the prayers.

Tension popped the beads out of his hand. He lost his place.

"Dammit," he mumbled. Pushing off the pew in front of him, he stood. He stumbled over the kneeler as he exited to the aisle. The dangling plastic of the rosary rattled against wood as his hands latched onto the curved pew rail to break his fall. The feel of the smooth, varnished mahogany recalled some seminal memory from childhood, a flash of calm entering him. Regaining his composure, he jammed the beads in his pants pocket and marched down the aisle.

Some other day, he thought.

Stepping into the bright early morning sunlight of Lagos, Dave bumped his way into the milling crowd on the street. An oil boom town of 21 million, the former Nigerian capital throbbed with humanity even at this early hour, every square block replete with perspiring obstacles, the un-sanitized, natural odors of their stale breath and sweaty clothing suffocating to Dave's American sensibilities in the stifling heat and humidity. Twisting between pedestrians who seemed to have no sense of urgency, he repeated a mantra of "excuse me." The people smiled broad grins, often with yellowed and broken teeth, each person responding with a polite "good morning," crowding closer together to make room.

Typically far less congested than other parts of Lagos, this neighborhood, an island separate from the heart of the city and lined with embassies, consulates, and the homes of Nigeria's richest families, had, until the last month, been quiet, filled with the sounds of birds, lawnmowers, and the cars of diplomats and government employees. Now, a ragged horde of refugees had arrived, crossing the bridges from the main part of the city or arriving by the poorest of boats. They pulsated over the manicured lawns, stripping the fruit off mango, lemon, and banana trees, many resorting to eating the fire-red flowers of the flamboyan trees. The odors of a dirty toilet mingled with the sweet fragrance of the fruit and flowers to affect an overwhelming contrast that found him unconsciously holding his breath.

Around him, people fleeing violence in the rural areas balanced woven baskets on their heads or lugged them on their shoulders, baskets that probably carried all their remaining possessions. An occasional goat, too skeletal to provide meat, tethered to a rope, held out the promise of a future meal as its owner urged it to feast on the thinning grass.

Seeking to escape the carnage that devastated their own humble communities, the refugees thought that neither the Boko Haram rebels nor the government would fire on the US Consulate and the streets surrounding it. No matter the outcome, the United States and the wealthy local business leaders would be needed by all sides.

The environment had no correlation to Dave's hometown of Fort Collins on Colorado's northern Front Range, a town straight out of the fifties sitcom *Leave it to Beaver* – at least on the surface. Disneyland's Main Street had been modeled after Fort Collins by a town native on Disney's staff in the 1950s. Lagos could never fit the Disney model.

But Dave's own background more closely resembled that of the refugees than that of the neighborhood's wealthy residents. For now, he had escaped his own past in a crowded red brick apartment building in Crafton, Pennsylvania. His father died in a traffic accident when he was ten, falling asleep at the wheel returning from the night shift at Jones & Laughlin Steel. After that, Dave started to mow lawns and deliver the Pittsburgh Press after school and weekends. His mother needed him to supplement her income as a checkout girl at the Giant Eagle grocery store down the street. He and his younger brother often lived on cans of tomato soup and chicken pot pies, picking apples from neighborhood trees for dessert. At school, kids laughed at their Salvation Army clothes, even though the clothes sometimes came from the Sears catalog on those rare occasions when their mother felt well off. When Mom couldn't make the rent, the small family even lived on cots in the basement of St. Philips Catholic Church for a few months until they built up enough reserves to rent another small apartment.

Dave never wanted to go back to that life and he never wanted Mel or Liv to experience it. Instead, he traveled to far corners of the world in pursuit of the big brass ring that had always been well out of reach for a working-class kid. He paid for good life insurance on himself, too. Just in case.

But now, he had a seat at the table with the silver spoon crowd. The stock options drove him. The potential upside if the company sold its stock in a public offering amounted to winning the lottery. Enough cash to pay for experimental uninsured treatments for Liv. And enough to allow him to retire and do whatever he and Mel wanted. Yet, for now, he did not even have enough in the bank to take off for three months – not if he wanted to pay for mortgages, car loans, and insurance, let alone special treatments for Liv.

So he kept pushing, focused on the initial public offering – the IPO, the Holy Grail, the big one-time event that could liberate him once and for all. As the company's VP of Operations and Business Development, he had the ball. He could make it happen within six to nine months, putting an end to his travel and non-stop work hours, the relentless purgatory he had endured for years.

He invested everything about himself in it. And, as he came to learn only in retrospect, he had risked everything.

Everything – and everyone – that mattered.

Two months earlier, he came home one evening to find his luggage on the front stoop and the locks changed. For over an hour, he negotiated and pleaded with Mel on his cell phone, shamelessly shedding tears while sitting hunched on the concrete steps. Crushed and humiliated – anger would come later – he moved into a motel by the interstate, setting up house with a laptop and a hot plate.

So he traveled. Before the separation, he would have been far more likely to delegate some of the travel to his employees. Mel had not been happy about his decision to take the job in the first place. She kept waiting for his workaholism to wind down, not up. Now, she claimed that Liv, just turned 15, hardly knew him; he certainly did not know her, she asserted.

"When is enough going to be enough for you?" she would ask as he came home to a house he sometimes had not seen in weeks.

Then, Liv's HIV diagnosis pushed everything over the edge. For all of them.

He had not been alone with Liv since the split, Mel fiercely holding on to custody. Yet he wanted to be with her more than ever. Mel relied on that. He had seen Liv only briefly at the lawyer's and Mel insisted on being present. When he had asked Liv questions, she looked to Mel for approval with each answer, restricting herself to safe one-word responses. But as he left, she threw her arms around him and whispered, "I love you, Daddy." He felt her wet tears on his cheek. He wanted to hold on to her forever, to make things better. Mel jerked her away.

Someone jostled him. Then, someone else. Instinctively, he grabbed his front pants pocket to protect his wallet and passport. Lagos. Don't daydream on the streets of Lagos, he thought.

A skinny teenage mother pushed a little boy and a little girl past him. "You go brush your teeth," she commanded. A teenager barely older than Liv, she looked much too young to have children that looked four or five. The children continued to laugh and poke at each other as the mother continued to propel them along.

"You go now," the mother repeated.

Remarkable, Dave thought. Her concern for dental hygiene in the middle of this hell impressed and surprised him. The girl must have come from a well-to-do family in one of the embattled areas. He tried to see her teeth, one of the indicators of social status, but she kept her determined lips tightly together as she hitched her basket further up her shoulder.

Without verbal response, the tiny brother and sister ran ahead to the front lawn of the nearest home dodging the spray from lawn sprinklers. There, they put toothpaste on their brushes like mini-adults. They leaned into one of the sprinklers and then spit foaming toothpaste at each other, giggling uncontrollably. Liv's laughter echoed in Dave's head, a smile crossing his face as he closed his eyes.

Shouts erupted from the crowd. A whistling sound. A blast concussion erupted from behind one of the houses. Dave leapt to the ground; others followed, landing on him and each other. To his right, the children looked up from the sprinkler. Panic crossed the boy's face, his brown eyes wide, his tiny hands reaching out to his mother across the yard.

Suddenly, he and his sister disappeared in a rain of dirt, smoke, and shrapnel. The concussion stunned Dave's eardrums into eerie silence. He lifted his head; it felt heavy. The young mother screamed silently as she raced over the grass, stepping over prone bodies that awaited the next mortar.

CHAPTER 3

Fort Collins, Clement Home
October 14, 11:11 p.m. Mountain Time

Mel Clement cracked the door to her daughter's room. Sound asleep, she thought. Thank God.

She walked down the hall to Liv's bathroom and opened the medicine cabinet. She took out three prescription bottles and sat on the toilet. She laid out a clean hand towel on the vanity and emptied each pill bottle one at a time. She carefully counted them to make sure the counts of each one matched the other two. They did. Then she looked at the dates on the bottles which also matched. Mentally calculating, she figured that there should be nine doses left of the drug cocktail prescribed for Liv.

There were only four remaining, five doses short.

That explains things, she thought. Liv, who Mel considered a little obsessive-compulsive, must have taken five double doses in the last several weeks. She could picture her thinking she had forgotten to take her dose and panicking. Liv would rush to the bathroom and take the next three pills, not thinking through whether or not she had actually skipped the dose earlier. A double dose could easily lead to hallucinations, especially when mixed with a hypnotic like Ambien.

Mel put the pills back in their respective bottles. She decided to keep the pills in her bathroom and personally administer them to Liv. Liv had insisted she not do it, but Mel thought the hallucinations dangerous. Making certain Liv only took the proper dosage would fix that.

As she placed the bottles in her own medicine cabinet a few minutes later, Mel looked at the drug names on them. She still struggled with disbelief that her 15 year old required anti-retrovirals. And Liv insisted she had never even been kissed. The science made no sense since HIV could only be transmitted through sexual encounters or blood transfusion, but still Mel believed her. Dave, on the other hand, insisted that one or the other had happened. And Liv had never had a blood transfusion. At least he did not accuse Liv to her face. Mel would not allow that. He reminded Mel that he worked in medical research. He argued that he knew the science. Well, he did not know his daughter as far as Mel was concerned.

Mel knew he was not mean about it. She could see the hurt in him, hurt for their family and hurt for what Liv faced. But he insisted to Mel that there had to have been some indiscretion. That angered her.

And he wonders why I threw him out, she thought.

CHAPTER 4

Lagos, Nigeria
October 15, 7:12 a.m. West Africa Time (WAT)

Dave stumbled toward the children, waving his arms in a futile effort to clear the thick smoke. Blinking his stinging eyes, he could make out the tiny bodies of the sister and brother flung together like rag dolls on the edge of the bomb crater. The mother pushed past him as others shoved him and pounded his back with fists.

"Go away, Oyinbo!" one shouted at him, invoking the local name for white man as an insult. But Dave could barely hear it, his eardrums still ringing from the blast. "You caused this," another yelled. Through the fog, Dave saw the mother throw herself at her children, embracing them, screaming for help.

A tall Nigerian man with close-cropped gray curls grabbed his arm and yanked him close. "Get out now," he shouted in his ear. "They're confused and frightened. They'll blame your skin and your clothes."

"It doesn't make sense. I want to help."

"Sense? What's wrong with you, man? For God's sake, just go."

Another mortar came, exploding about thirty yards behind him in the street. This time, Dave did not hit the ground. In front of him, he saw a mix of wailing and angry faces. They would not let him help. Not an Oyinbo. Not here. Not in this moment.

Another blast. Closer. Fear surged through him. He began running, weaving through pedestrians like a halfback, he raced for the US consulate, nearly a mile away.

When he arrived, a mass of people throbbed around the consulate's gate. Dave pushed his way through the panicked Nigerians. As he neared the front of the pack, a pungent stench filled his nose. At first, he thought it came from the people in the pack, but it grew stronger as he drew closer to the gate. With a final shoulder nudge, he reached the gate with its closely placed iron bars. On the other side, five young Marines in dress blues, brass buttons glittering in the sun, stood out of reach of pleading arms. The Marines' eyes reflected repulsion, fear, and confusion. One of them spoke on a phone asking for guidance. At the foot of the gate lay a ragged stack of eight dead Nigerian civilians with open wounds. The Nigerians pleading at the gate sought burial for their loved ones. Somehow, the rumor had spread that these uniformed Americans had the means and the intent to assist.

Gasping, Dave inadvertently inhaled a deep breath of the wretched air, swallowing a gulp of the acrid intestinal gasses emanating from the rotting bodies. He gagged on a rush of vomit he barely kept down. As he backed out of the crowd, one of the Marines looked to him for help. Dave turned away, bumped his way through the crowd, and began jogging. For once pleased with the strong exhaust fumes that helped mask the taste of death in his mouth, he sucked in the thick city air. As his pace accelerated, he broke into a sweat that soaked his button-down shirt and slacks, pooling in his shoes by the time he reached the hospital.

The temporary hospital compound set up by Mèdecins Sans Frontiéres (MSF), known as Doctors Without Borders in the United States, consisted of a large home and a separate cottage. Formerly a private residence, it had been donated by a wealthy supporter of the French-founded charity. Just six months earlier, it had been where volunteering doctors and nurses came for orientation before heading out to the bush for weeks or months. Two pristine, white-washed buildings occupied grounds of precisely manicured lawns with thick blades of green grass, the kind that felt cool and soft beneath the tread of bare feet. Urgent need and self-sacrifice had caused the doctors to convert their home and safe haven. Now, under once carefully trimmed trees, sick and frightened people competed for shade, completely obscuring the lawn, much of it worn to red dirt after weeks of wounded passing through.

A mass of shouting Nigerians pressed against the front entrance blocking Dave's path. The scene resembled the one at the consulate – without the Marines. He knew the back entrance and sought it out.

The back of the building housed the triage unit, formerly the great room. Every conceivable option for a bed had been used to make room for the wounded. In the midst of the bodies, Dave, still catching his breath, saw Adrian Guerra standing. The lanky Guerra, the West African Country Director for the World Bank, afforded Dave only a glance from beneath unkempt salt-and-pepper hair. Guerra carried colored tags identifying treatment for the victims. Dave watched Guerra affix a black toe tag on a young girl laid across empty fruit crates. Cued by the tag, the medical staff would rush by the child, focused on other cases with more hope.

Guerra moved from patient to patient as the doctors assessed each victim. Sucking in a deep breath, Dave, still dripping sweat, walked up to him.

"Tough duty," Dave said. "How'd you get recruited?"

"The director and I were having coffee upstairs when today's first wave came in. They needed extra hands."

Dave looked around the room to see how he might help. Confusion reigned as more wounded arrived.

Guerra noted the sweat soaking Dave's clothes. "I thought you'd already be in Freetown to see your missionary friend, not running a race," he said, attaching a green toe tag, giving hope to a young man still in his school uniform.

"What's your name, son?" Guerra asked.

"Gerard," the boy squeaked.

"We're going to take good care of you, Gerard."

"When do you fly to Freetown?" Guerra asked Dave.

"Tomorrow morning." Dave looked at the boy, wondering how much could be done about the gaping wound on the far right side of his chest.

"Good, turns out we're on the same flight. No deals here, right?"

"I told you at the reception last night. I won't agree to anything until I see all the data."

"Give me a break, Dave. Do you think you can deploy PDNAs with any control in this environment? The Boko Haram are lobbing mortars onto Victoria Island, for God's sake. No one ever thought they'd have the audacity to attack this part of Lagos. Or the capacity."

"I thought they were isolated in the north."

"Not any more. This is definitely their handiwork." Guerra gestured toward the sea of patients. "I swapped emails with Claire McQuaid at the Aldrich Institute. She doesn't want to waste the malaria vaccine investment here. She wants to focus on Sierra Leone. We need your PDNAs there, not here."

"I'm open to change, Adrian, but the Nigerians need the PDNAs. They can help disprove this bull about the polio vaccine being some kind of Trojan horse for AIDS and infertility."

"Claire's obsessive and maybe a little crazy, Dave. I'd do things her way." Guerra managed the World Bank's liaison office in Freetown, Sierra Leone. He had traveled down to Lagos specifically to pre-empt Dave's option to deploy the first portable DNA analyzers (PDNAs) in Nigeria. Dave had made up his mind that his PDNA could fix the mis-perceptions in Nigeria. Adrian, Claire and even Jennifer in Dave's office, told him it was the wrong place at the wrong time. But he was hard-headed.

Guerra shrugged his shoulders. "This country's in bad shape. It's religious politics. The Muslims hate the Christians and the Christians hate the Muslims. If anyone doesn't feel that way, someone will kill their relative tomorrow and push them over the edge. It's not about truth or God at all. It's about greedy boys on all sides using religion to seize power."

"Sierra Leone has its own issues," Dave said. "Since the Ebola crisis, it's been set back at least five years."

"But it's fairly stable. And we need stability for a demonstration project. Talk to your priest friend in Freetown. He'll tell you. A few stray rebel and criminal bands left in the boonies aren't an issue. The civil war's over in Sierra Leone. You can do some good up there with an early launch of the malaria vaccine pilot. Can you say that about this place? We're in the warm-up stages here. The country's breaking in two, Muslims in the north, Christians in the south. And the south is where the oil is. It's fragile as hell."

Dave did not answer. He wanted to do what was right. He had a history with Fr. Jim Reilly, and helping out in Sierra Leone held a lot of appeal. But when he submitted the original assessment to the World Health Organization aka WHO, Nigeria enjoyed stability, not Sierra Leone. Changing the assessment would mean a pile of paperwork and getting Evan Conger, WHO's director for sub-tropical diseases, signed up. Dave knew, however, that Evan, his long-time mentor, would probably support whatever recommendation he made. At Dave's request, Evan would be joining Dave and Adrian in Sierra Leone in the morning.

Passing among the wounded, Dave jerked his face away from a bowel spilling on to a desktop. A solemn doctor mumbled "black" to Adrian. Steeling himself, Dave touched the dying man's ankle and very quietly mumbled a prayer.

Adrian leaned close to Dave's ear, whispering. "You're wasting your time."

"Why?"

"You think that a good God would let this crap happen?" Showing resignation, not anger, Adrian's eyes lingered on Dave.

Dave did not have Sunday School answers for this situation, but he survived on hope, sometimes more fumes than substance. For much of his life, he had only that. He lifted a silent prayer that the victims not experience the same kind of despair as Adrian Guerra.

"Stop it, man," Adrian whispered, seeing Dave briefly lift his eyes to the ceiling.

"How can we do this to each other?"

"Really? We'll talk on the plane tomorrow," Adrian said.

Dave nodded. Adrian placed another black tag.

"How can I help?" Dave asked.

"You should see the woman doc in the dining room," Adrian suggested. "I think you know her from the infectious disease conference in San Diego. This toe-tagging's a one-man job."

Maneuvering around makeshift gurneys, Dave reached the doctor coordinating the activities. "Hi, Sharon," he said, reaching out a hand. "Doesn't get much worse."

"PDNAs won't help any of this, will they?" she said as she finished writing a note. "What are you doing here? Your wife will kill you if you ruin those clothes." She forced a half-smile.

Dave did not explain about his marriage. "There are more important things than my clothes," he said.

Sharon nodded. "Thanks," she said. "We can use all the able bodies we can find. I have a serious problem on the other side. You'll need to recruit some locals to help you. We can't leave the dead piling up at the main entrance. It's a recipe for epidemic."

Alarm registered on his face.

"Never mind. That's not fair of me. You don't need that. There are plenty of other jobs to do. How about…"

The teenage mother's wails echoed in his mind. "No. I'll do it. Where do I put the…ah…?"

"The dead. No time to worry about political correctness here."

"So where do I put them, Sharon?"

"I wish I knew. We need a makeshift morgue. The room we've been using is too small. It has patients in it now, anyway. Be creative. Try the consulate. I hear you can get asylum if you're dead."

"Been there. It's a lie." Dave started to walk away.

"Yo, Dave!"

He turned just in time to catch a handful of loose items thrown at him.

"You'll need those," she said.

He looked at the sterile gloves and surgical mask in his hands.

"Thanks again," she said. "Keep this crap up and you'll be dead from something exotic within the year." She winked.

He headed for the bodies. Dead within a year, he thought. Since Mel threw him out, he had dark moments when that did not seem to be soon enough. The Black Dog, Winston Churchill called it. The bleak despair revealed in his mother's wet eyes still haunted him decades later, an image of a yellow eviction sticker affixed to the door closed behind them as they abandoned another apartment. He fought the quiet urge to die, to drift into sleep and never wake up. For years, only faith kept this haunting at bay until Mel's love finally broke its hold – its demise cemented by Liv's birth. Until now.

At the doorway, he affixed the surgical mask and kept his mouth tightly shut. Still, the pungent odor of human decay penetrated, stinging his tongue as though it had been plunged in a septic tank. He longed for a spray can of deodorizer.

The surrounding crowd cried out with pleadings, not hostilities. As with the American consulate, word had gone out that the hospital would find a way to properly bury their loved ones. Organizing them to be claimed and buried now fell on Dave's shoulders. The backyard of the compound had enough open space for a temporary alternative, weather permitting.

He looked at the broken bodies caked with mud and blood. It surprised him to see elderly people and children among those in the pile. His intellect knew they would be there. His spirit struggled with it. He gazed over them, most of their bodies contorted in agony, some of their faces frozen in horrified surprise.

Dead within a year, he again pondered. How many of them thought they would be gone within the year?

He pulled on the gloves, tossed a handful of body bags over his shoulder, and plunged into the crowd of the living to seek recruits.

CHAPTER 5

Lokoma Village, Sierra Leone, Northwestern Mountains –
1,150 miles west of Lagos
October 15, 3 p.m. Greenwich Mean Time

A powerful gust of wind bent tree limbs and whipped leaves through the congregation. Above them, the bloated fingers of billowing black thunderheads devoured the light of the morning sun. Father Jim Reilly planted his right knee firmly in the thick damp grass of the small clearing, genuflecting before the portable altar. Lightning flashed through the rainforest canopy as he stood back up. A loud explosion of thunder followed less than two seconds later. The missionary's parishioners stole quick glances at one another seeking reassurance that the thunder was not mortar fire.

Holding the gold-plated ciborium containing the hosts in one hand, Jim wiped his brow with the back of the other in an effort to keep the stinging sweat from his eyes. His white vestments, trimmed in shamrock green, had been drenched since early in the short weekday Mass. He found the humidity of Sierra Leone even more intense than he experienced as a boy at the monastery outside of Augusta, Georgia. There, he had been concealed under a new identity for years after escaping retribution in Northern Ireland. Decades later, both the Irish Republican Army and the opposing Protestant Loyalist Volunteer Force still had murder contracts out on him. His hot and stuffy vestments amounted to a small penance to pay for anonymity.

Cast in the glimmering gray-green pall that heralded an imminent storm, he nodded for the Lokoma village congregation to come forward to receive Communion. Jacob Karanja, his altar server and son of the tribe's chief, stood before him in white surplice and black cassock, opening his hands to be the first to accept the host today. At just under five feet tall, the bony wide-eyed boy barely stood as high as the tall priest's elbow.

"Body of Christ," Jim said, his Irish brogue still easily detected.

"Amen," the ten year old responded, muddy feet and sandals peering out below his cassock. He picked the host out of his hand and placed it on his tongue.

A jagged lightning bolt hurtled across the darkening sky that etched the wind-tossed tree line behind the altar. An ear-splitting thunderclap followed within a second this time. Jim was running out of time as the storm closed in. He tried to focus on the body and blood of Jesus as he placed a host in the hands of each of the congregants that stepped forward. Yet almost every time Jesus came into focus, Jim inevitably remembered his own failings as he pondered the mystery of God's forgiveness. Here and in his daily life, he worked very hard to center in God, to not be distracted by the world. But sometimes, distraction helped him. Forgetting could provide interludes of peace for a man keenly aware of the deadly harm he had done.

Another blast. Not as loud. And much further away. Mortar fire.

The priest and the villagers stood silently for a moment. Jim waited thirty seconds and heard no more mortar fire. With multiple factions constantly competing for territory, random explosions in the distance had been commonplace in Sierra Leone for more than a decade. Jim resumed the distribution of hosts.

As he finished with the last person, a streak of lightning saturated the clearing with blinding white light. A nearly simultaneous thunderclap erupted in the forest. The villagers flinched slightly, but otherwise they remained calmly standing, their eyes glancing in the direction of the sound, tensely waiting for Jim to finish Mass.

Almost as much as the immediate threat, the mortar fire concerned Jim in a more universal way. He and Hamara Karanja, the village chief, needed to present the village as a safe area, hoping to persuade Dave Clement, Jim's long-time friend, to bring the malaria vaccine demonstration project to Lokoma. The years of fighting in the small country had, in fact, left the isolated village intact, threatened on several occasions with nearby explosions and gunfire but never actually experiencing invasion or a direct hit. The surrender of the central rebel leadership had tempered the threat, but isolated remnants of the rebels continued to operate, becoming unorganized and opportunistic marauders. The central government in Freetown would not help, instead focusing its limited resources on the cities. As long as the bandits and rebels stayed out of the urban centers, the government looked away while random violence continued in the rural mountains and rainforest.

Jim urgently cleaned the gold-plated chalice and the ciborium. He locked them in their case. To protect them from the elements, he placed the chalice case and his sacramentary, the thick book containing the prayers of the Mass, in a small cooler. He faced the villagers.

"May almighty God bless you, the Father, and the Son, and the Holy Spirit," he said as he made the sign of the cross over the congregation.

"Amen," they replied in unison.

"Go in the peace of Christ."

"Thanks be to God."

A deafening crash exploded on top of them as lightning split a nearby tree. A torrent of rain suddenly poured down. The villagers shouted to each other, running under the tree canopy for shelter. Then, another mortar exploded in the midst of the deluge. Closer than before. Then another explosion. Closer still. And another even closer. Screams erupted from the crowd and people raced back toward the village less than a hundred yards away. Only Jacob stood his ground with the priest, latching on to him with his hand.

"Take your surplice and cassock off, Jacob," Jim ordered. Both men pulled the vestments over their heads, revealing their street clothes. The priest quickly folded the wet vestments and shoved them into the cooler. He listened as the mortar fire continued. He decided the bandits were "walking" the mortar fire toward the clearing, calibrating their aim.

Not now, he thought. Not when the Lokoma finally had a shot at beating malaria. Dave Clement would never be able to justify bringing the vaccine project to the tribe if they had an incident now. Worse yet, if this was a full scale assault, Lokoma villagers would die.

The cloudburst stopped. "Don't let them come here now," he prayed quietly, lifting his eyes heavenward toward the still roiling thunderheads.

He turned toward Jacob who looked even smaller in his shorts and t-shirt than he did in his altar boy vestments. "You can run home, Jacob. It's not safe here."

"A chief's son never runs."

"Then stay close." Jim had known the boy since he was an infant, supported him and his family through an early illness, ultimately baptizing him with the chief and many others a few years earlier. He worried about him as though he were his own son. Jacob still hurt from the loss of his seven-year-old sister Ketta to malaria four months earlier, a sister the boy had treated badly at times. Now, Jacob seemed to compensate by catering to five-year-old Sara. In his overprotective zeal, he had once even insisted on tasting her food first.

"I think it's stopped, Father," Jacob said.

Jim heard only the rumble of thunder and rain dripping from the trees. No more mortar fire. Then, he heard the grinding of gears and the struggling engine of an old truck coming up the road that paralleled the clearing. A horn honked. A rusted flatbed spewing diesel fumes rumbled over the rutted trail. Chief Hamara Karanja threw open the passenger door to let in his son. Jacob scrambled up into the cab.

"How de body, Father?" Hamara said.

"Bein' good," Jim responded. "Join ya?"

"Happy to have ya. We need to find out who this is and try to steer them in a different direction. We have a big day tomorrow." Hamara waved a 12 gauge shotgun at him.

"Tomorrow's meeting won't matter if the village is attacked," Jim said, wondering how the chief thought he could use a shotgun to bluff bandits with AK-47s.

Jim threw the cooler containing the sacred objects and vestments behind the seat. He squeezed into the passenger side. The truck jerked forward as Hamara thrust it into gear. Seconds later, another mortar explosion sounded, this one very close. Hamara leaned into the steering wheel, scanning for any movement.

"I can't see anything," he said.

"Pull over, Chief. I'll climb onto the back for a better view."

Hamara stopped the truck. Jim clambered out and into the flatbed. Hamara drove on. As the truck ground back into a driving gear, the priest tightly gripped the splintered wooden rail surrounding the bed.

Accelerating, the old farm truck swerved, bouncing violently over the dirt road to avoid a deep rut. Small arms fire crackled in the forest ahead. Jim leaned toward the driver's window as a slight drizzle started. Overhead, thunder continued to rumble.

The Lokoma, had only a few shotguns, bows and arrows, machetes, and knives to defend themselves. The villagers did not seem a logical target. They had nothing to steal. Since their jobs in bauxite mining on the neighboring plateau went away during the war, they were nothing more than hunters and subsistence farmers. They kept to themselves, territorially unambitious and self-sufficient.

Another mortar blast, the impact less than twenty yards away. The concussion wave slammed into Jim, knocking him backward onto the truck's bed.

"You okay, Father?" Jacob called, leaning halfway out the passenger window.

Jim did not answer. Rolling to the edge, he instinctively grabbed a rail. The rain suddenly came down again in sheets. A series of lightning strikes detonated convulsively in the forest around them.

"Papa, stop!"

"I'm okay," Jim called as he settled himself more securely on the rocking bed of the truck. He held a hand over his brow to block the rain. Something ahead caught his eye. He pulled himself up to the cab for a better look. Boys close to Jacob's age raced across the road just over a rise less than 50 yards ahead. Clad in t-shirts and shorts, some with bandoliers over their shoulders, they looked like an elementary-school class playing at war, but every one of them carried real Kalashnikov AK-47s as long as many of the boys were tall. Jim banged on the roof of the truck to get Hamara's attention. The chief stopped the truck and leaned out the window.

"Turn it around, Chief! Bandits crossing the road just over that hill."

The chief jerked the gearshift into reverse, backing into the trees to turn around. As he did, bullets whistled overhead, splitting off splinters of branches that ricocheted off the truck. Jim flattened himself on the bed, hands covering his head. The gears ground painfully and noisily as Hamara struggled to get the vehicle moving.

A lightning bolt erupted in the direction of the bandits, violently rupturing a tree. Jim used the distraction to pull himself up on the truck's cab and peer through the downpour. Six boys close to Jacob's age raced toward the top of the hill. The sides of the truck thunked and pinged as more targeted fire erupted from the barrels of the boys' weapons. Hamara leaned on the gas, pulling away.

Cresting another hill, just out of the sight line of the child soldiers, the truck smashed into a new bomb crater, nearly turning over on its side, its driver-side wheels flinging mud as they spun uselessly in the air. Jim slammed against the side rail as his splintered hands slipped from their hold. The rail came loose and gashed his head, causing blood to spill down the right side of his face. The small of his back landed on the edge of the two-by-four rail, a loosened bolt drilling into a kidney.

Groaning, he rolled onto the ground, just eighteen inches below where he had sprawled on the nearly overturned vehicle. He pulled himself up and ran to Hamara's window. It stood nearly a head taller than Jim because of the truck's cockeyed angle in the bomb crater.

"You two all right?"

"Damn road!" cursed Hamara, his temples throbbing beneath the smatterings of gray on his short, coiled hair.

"We should run for it," Jim said, rain streaming down his face.

The Chief returned a determined look and showed the priest the shotgun again, cocking it as he did so.

"No you don't, Chief," Jim said, calculating the odds. Bullets whizzed overhead. If the child soldiers had the presence of mind to stop and take aim, death would be a certainty, he thought.

"Let's get Jacob out of here anyway," Jim shouted over the storm.

Hamara peered out the driver's window. "Long drop," the Chief called back. "If the truck tilts any further, Jacob could get crushed trying to go out the passenger side. I'll drop him down to you from here." He turned to his son. "Give me your hand, Jacob," Hamara instructed.

Inside the truck, Jacob latched on.

"Climb over me. Hurry!"

Using his father and the steering wheel for leverage, the small boy scrambled to the window of the driver's door. Jim stood below, waiting to catch him. Jacob jumped and the priest grasped him at the armpits, easing his flight to the ground.

A round skipped over the top of the cab. Jim pushed Jacob to the ground.

Hamara called down. "Jacob, lay down in a rut so you can't be seen. No argument." He raised his shotgun and directed it toward the attackers.

Bent over to stay below the line of sight of the rebel's weapons, Jim assessed the options. "Put that stupid thing down," the priest ordered. "I have a better idea. Start driving when I say go." Jim seized the broken rail. He wedged it between a rock and the suspended right rear tire to provide traction.

A round splintered the top of the truck bed's remaining rail. Leaves overhead rained down as bullets flew through them.

The priest raced around and placed his back under the passenger side of the cab, pushing back with all his might, his boots sinking into the clay.

"Go, Chief! Drive!" he yelled.

Hamara's left foot jumped off the clutch, his right foot slamming down on the gas. His right hand latched onto the black gearshift knob. He shifted back and forth between first and reverse as his feet danced on the pedals. Alternating between grinding and roaring, the truck rocked in search of footing.

Trying to use the momentum of the rocking to leverage his 230 pounds to right the vehicle, Jim strained backward against the cab with all the force he could muster, the veins bulging on his blood-red forehead and neck.

Nothing.

Jacob appeared beside him and began pushing on the cab with his hands.

"Jacob! Get back down!"

"You need help, Father," the boy shouted over the roar of the truck's churning engine, his sandals disappearing into the mud as he pushed.

The weapons fire continued relentlessly, now taking splinters out of the trees just a few inches over Jim's head.

"Pray with me, then," Jim said. "Hail Mary, full of grace, the Lord is with thee…"

Jacob joined in, leaning a shoulder into the truck, a grimace of determination on his face.

The truck rocked. First gear. Reverse. First gear. Reverse. First gear. Some give. Reverse. First gear. More give.

Hamara gunned it. In a single leap, the truck hurtled out of the crater, flinging red mud everywhere.

Jim and Jacob sprinted and leapt on to the truck bed, sprawling flat to provide smaller targets.

"Go! Go! Go!" Jim yelled.

"…pray for us sinners now and at the hour of our death amen," Jacob continued.

Both of them looked back. The heads of the lead boys appeared over the hill as the old truck accelerated, putting distance between them and the danger. The rain intensified and the boys instantly faded from view. In less than 20 seconds, the truck hurtled around a sharp bend in the road and out of their direct line of fire.

As the truck bounced further along through the muck, the gunfire slowed and then faded. Hamara braked to a stop, turning off the engine to listen. The chirping of birds and the stirring of leaves resonated around them. Like popcorn near the end of its cycle in a microwave, the rhythm of weapons fire slowed to sporadic pops, finally stopping completely. The village had not been the target. The Chief and Jim surmised a competing group had meant the mortar fire for the boy soldiers they had encountered. Now, the fighting had moved south and east, a near miss for Lokoma village, but a miss nonetheless. Like tornados, rebel attacks cut a narrow swath, devastating anything in their direct path, but leaving everything else untouched.

"Those rifles were bigger than those boys," Jacob observed.

"They were indeed," Jim said.

"I need one," the boy said.

"No, Jacob. You don't."

Jacob stared at the priest for a moment, and then looked away into the rain, now a gentle shower.

Lokoma Village
October 16, 2:30 a.m. Greenwich Mean Time

Fr. Jim rarely spent nights in a village, preferring to get back to his small apartment in Freetown, but he wanted to be there early in the morning to welcome Dave Clement and his entourage. So he chose instead to stay and lead the Lokoma in an evening benediction and rosary in thanksgiving for the village again escaping violence.

As he wrestled with sleep, the futon in the small hut offered no cushion for his big frame, but it put a barrier between him and whatever might be dwelling in the dirt floor beneath.

Recently, sleep had been coming more readily to him, but the day's explosions kept ringing in his ears, even as he finally nodded off.

Jim found himself drawn to the carnage. Silhouetted by flames, roasting forms shriveled in the back seat, their humanity already barely discernible. A piece of white dress, one edge aflame, lay on the cobblestones, just steps from him. Gasping, his ears popped.

"...bloody idiot!" a boy shouted.

The anguished wails of a man pierced the nightmare. Then Jim saw him. Bleeding, one pant leg dragging and misshapen, the man crawled close to the flames and twisted metal.

Repelled by the heat, he latched on to a tiny white shoe blown into the cobblestones...

Jim awoke sweating. At first, he thought the heat came from the flames, not the jungle. He rolled onto his side and slapped a hand into the dirt beside the futon. His fingers dug into the earth as though it would wipe the images from his mind. Wide-eyed, he peered into the darkness of the hut and began mumbling a Hail Mary.

CHAPTER 6

Clement Home
October 15, 8 p.m. Mountain Daylight Time

Mel sat with Liv in the family room watching a reality show about a songwriting competition. Liv enjoyed the music, aspiring to be a songwriter herself. Mel liked that it distracted her. After last night, she did not want her out of her sight until she was ready to pass out from sleep. Liv's phone sat on the end table beside Mel. It held no threatening texts. Liv could not explain why they were missing. She seemed genuinely surprised that they were missing. Mel doubted the texts ever existed, preferring to believe Liv experienced pharmaceutically-induced hallucinations, not a stalker.

When the sun set two hours earlier, Mel closed all the blinds in the family room. Just in case. Liv watched her approvingly.

As Liv pressed the remote to fast-forward through commercials, she turned to her mother. "I didn't imagine it, Mom."

Mel pondered a response for a good 15 seconds before speaking. "The drugs are strong. It's all right if they make you see things."

"I wish that was it. I can tell the difference between reality and fantasy."

"I'd prefer that you couldn't. We can change drugs."

"We can stop my stalker, too." Liv picked up a sharp kitchen knife off the edge of the couch where she had placed it earlier. Her pupils widened; her neck and face flushed.

Mel placed a hand on her daughter's arm and gently guided the knife back down to the couch. "That's more likely to hurt us than an intruder," she said.

Liv pursed her lips, blinking back a tear. "You need to let Dad move back home," she said.

Mel picked up the knife and carried it back to the kitchen on the far end of the family room. She opened the refrigerator as she called back to Liv, "Do you want a diet soda?"

CHAPTER 7

Victoria Crown Plaza Hotel, Lagos
October 16, 4:17 a.m. West African Time

Adrian Guerra reached for the vibration on the bedside stand. "What the hell," he mumbled as he picked up his phone. He saw a text from Claire McQuaid in Boulder.

> Status?

"Really? Now?" he said into the dark room. Rolling on to his back, he yawned and then sat up to tap his response.

> Dave Clement behaving - if that's what you mean.

Claire fired back in seconds:

> Did he show any signs of misbehavior?

Misbehavior? thought Adrian. He tried to put Claire's mind at ease and quickly tapped back:

> A boy scout.

> Too bad. Keep him close. He's essential.

> OK

> Get some sleep.

"Right," he said out loud as he dropped back down flat on the hotel bed. "You are one serious control freak, lady."

He looked at the time on his phone and then slammed the phone down on the bed. 4:20 a.m. He would never get back to sleep now. And he had a plane to catch. Poor Dave, he thought. Claire had the man in her crosshairs. That could not possibly be fun. Or safe.

CHAPTER 8

Lokoma Village, Sierra Leone
October 16, 7:50 a.m. Greenwich Mean Time

Dave's thin khaki shirt stuck to his body and chafed even though it was not tucked in. In the muggy heat, the sweat from the band of his wide-brimmed straw hat seeped over his brow. He swatted gnats and mosquitoes as he stood amidst single story mud-walled buildings with thatch roofs in the dusty center of quiet Lokoma village in the hilly rainforest southeast of Freetown, Sierra Leone.

The rich perfume of yellow tropical blossoms mingled with the odor of animal manure and of people without running water. The trench latrine twenty yards behind the closest building emitted the stink of warm human waste. The stale smells of extinguished cooking fires provided an undercurrent to the stronger smells. In mid-afternoon, meal preparation would supplant them all with the enticing aromas of fresh food.

Goats, dogs, chickens, pigs, and children wandered aimlessly over the village's irregular dirt road. Springing from the road, a spider web of paths, defined primarily by trampled foliage, led between short mud buildings into the overgrown jungle. The animals left droppings wherever nature called, making it imperative to pay attention as one walked. Preoccupied with rummaging for food, the animals ignored the pops of distant gunfire that had started again just after dawn. The children ignored it as well, caught up in chasing each other or taunting animals.

The people studied Dave and his companions curiously, smiling brightly when he caught them looking. Omnipresent parasites in their bellies, not obesity, gave many of them a bloated look. Parasites and worms invaded through cracks in their toes, through the water and the food supply, sometimes through the air. Dave had never wormed himself before traveling in this region; now he often conducted a worming routine upon returning to the United States, particularly if he had spent any time in the bush.

Accompanied by Evan Conger from the World Health Organization and Adrian Guerra, Dave expected this visit to result in consensus on where to deploy the malaria vaccine and the PDNAs. On the drive from Freetown, Dave and Adrian proposed to Evan that they switch the program from Nigeria to Sierra Leone. Evan agreed to smooth the path with WHO, pending the outcome of today's visit.

A mentor to Dave, Evan had recommended him for the Prodeus job. In his mid-sixties, Evan bore the chiseled features of a patrician and a full head of snow-white hair. He headed the World Health Organization's sub-Saharan vaccination program. He had started the malaria vaccine development while executive director for the Aldrich Institute in Boulder, leaving early in the project when the President called on him to be US Surgeon General. After two years in that slot, the administration lost the White House, freeing Evan to do meaningful work at a senior level for WHO, a lifelong dream. Through WHO, he hoped to finally deploy the malaria vaccine he had set in motion while in Boulder.

His successor at the Aldrich, Claire McQuaid, assured Evan the vaccine would be through initial clinical trials and ready for deployment in a WHO certified demonstration project within months. While the US Food and Drug Administration might take years to approve the vaccine, Sierra Leone's health minister, William Tombu, had very little bureaucracy to overcome and no qualms about bringing the vaccine in as soon as limited clinical trials declared it viable. Minister Tombu, McQuaid, and Evan all believed that too many lives could be lost while waiting to dot the "i's" and cross the "t's."

Hamara Karanja and Fr. Jim escorted the men to chairs under a giant banyan tree that provided the only shade in the village center. The chief shooshed away animals and children. Several rounds of gunfire went off in the distance.

"Should we be concerned?" Dave asked.

"All well," Hamara answered, using a local Krio idiom. "The terrain makes it sound much closer than it really is."

They sat down and women brought them tea, a single ice cube and a four-inch stick of raw sugar cane placed in each cup. Evan introduced the subject of the visit. "Chief, we think the Lokoma tribe is a good candidate to test a new malaria vaccine. With your authorization, we'd like to provide it to your people."

"Does it work?"

"It does."

"What would need to do in exchange?"

"Not a lot. We want to keep this easy for you. We'll carry the burden of the implementation. All the medical staffing will be provided by a team coordinated by Sierra Leone's ministry of health and the Aldrich Institute. The World Bank and W-H-O will take care of any funding requirements. You just need to say yes."

"It's not always easy to trust outsiders who come here," the chief said.

"I understand," Evan said. "We have to earn that right."

Adrian Guerra leaned forward in his seat. "I represent the World Bank. Large, well-financed and very interested in the well-being of your people. Plus you know me."

Hamara's looked at Adrian, his face expressionless. "I do know you, Adrian. That's my point." He turned his attention to Dave.

"You're working with these men, Dave. Are there safeguards and enough incentive for them to prioritize the interests of our tribe?"

"Listen, Chief," Adrian interrupted.

Hamara held a hand up to Adrian. "I asked Dave," he said."

Dave struggled to keep from smiling. Adrian annoyed him. He liked that Hamara could manage him. "Yes," he said. "Everyone's interests are aligned. The success of the vaccine with the demonstration site, Lokoma in this case, is essential to everyone's interests."

"That's all I need," said Hamara. "How do we get started?"

"I'm not sure what just happened," Adrian said.

Fr. Jim smiled. "Don't take it too personally. There's history behind the Chief's confidence. Years ago, I spoke at Dave's church in Colorado on a fundraising tour. He and Mel stepped up in a big way."

Hamara reached into his shirt pocket and pulled out a pair of glasses. "I read with these. The Clements paid for hundreds of them. Only a very few of us ever had that luxury before."

Adrian raised his eyebrows and nodded.

"Well, we hope to work with Dave to do even more going forward," Evan said as he re-entered the conversation. "He and I discussed the options on the drive up. The initial proposal put the program in Nigeria, but there's a compelling case to start here."

Hamara stirred his tea with the sugar cane stick. "Where else have you tested?"

"We had a good outcome in a small clinical trial with the Kuna in Panama," Evan began to explain the data from the Kuna study and to disclose some of the uncertainties.

Hamara interrupted him. "When can you have it here?"

"Within two months," he answered. "We're concerned, however, about the potential for violence. That would undermine the test and deny everyone the vaccine."

"We understand," Hamara said. "What happened in Nigeria is not likely to happen here. But it could. With the wrong kind of publicity. So it pays to be careful."

"You read my mind," Evan said. "That's where Dave's company comes in."

"We think the key is to be pro-active," Dave said on cue. He took a quick swallow of his tea. It tasted of ginger, something the Lokoma added to fight parasites in the digestive tract. "I'm probably telling you something you already know, but whole towns in Nigeria have not been vaccinated for polio. Radical imams in the north claim the vaccine carries HIV and makes women infertile. They've convinced people that it's a western plot. Truckloads of polio vaccine have been hijacked and destroyed. Dozens of aid workers have been slaughtered. And thousands of children are getting polio."

Hamara circled his hands around his cup as he spoke. "I won't claim that we don't have issues here, but our nation is weary of war. In Nigeria, they're fighting for control of the oil wealth. We don't have that in Sierra Leone."

He finished with an idiom. "If God agree, we never will."

A tiny barefoot girl ran up to him and jumped into his arms. A broad white smile covered her chocolate face, big brown eyes shining with excitement. Wearing only a bright blue t-shirt that hung down to her knees, she squeezed Hamara's neck and then leaned back. She ran her tiny fingers around his face.

"Are they here to stop the guns, Papa?" she asked. "Mama and I prayed when we heard the guns."

He pulled her close and gently stroked her back. "The guns are far away, sweet girl. They won't hurt us. These men came to help fight sickness."

"Like Ketta's?"

The chief nodded solemnly as he pulled her into his lap. She inspected the men whose eyes fixated on her.

"Gentlemen, this is Sara, one of the loves of my life."

"You don't remember me, Sara, but I remember you," Dave said.

The little girl shook her head and grinned.

"Do you know his face, Sara?" Hamara said.

She grinned wider and pressed her nose into her father's shoulder.

"She was too young to remember when you came with your family," the Chief said. "But she recognizes you from a picture of that visit."

"How old are you now, Sara?" Dave asked.

Sara looked down and to the side. She held up five tiny fingers. An image of a much younger Liv flashed in Dave's mind.

"So how do you prevent the conspiracy rumors, Dave?" Hamara asked as he gently bounced Sara in his lap.

"With a portable DNA analyzer. The PDNA samples DNA and blood drawn both before and after the vaccine inoculation. The first blood draw identifies who has HIV before the vaccination. The second draw, after the vaccination is administered, confirms that the vaccine hasn't changed any of that. It proves that we're stopping disease, not injecting people with it."

Hamara thought for a moment. "I like it. A little cloak and dagger, but I like it."

"There's a good medical reason, too. The PDNA also tells us which DNA profiles are most vulnerable to malaria and which will respond well to the vaccine."

"Then the vaccine works better for some than others?"

"Right. Because it attacks disease at the genetic level and each of us has a different genetic make-up."

"I don't like that. How many will be eligible?"

"Eventually, everyone. But, for now, we expect to help about seventy percent."

Hamara thought for a moment. "Okay. That's seventy percent more than today."

"It's a good start."

Hamara responded with another Krio idiom. "We tell God tank for dat."

"We'll need your help getting public support," Dave said. "From both you and Father Jim. This region will respond to the two of you – and trust you. If you tell them the vaccine is sound, people will believe it. If false rumors start to circulate, we'll give you the data to disprove them."

Hamara's eyes narrowed. "What kind of data?"

"It's all in the blood samples and the PDNA results. You'll have a verifiable before-and-after snapshot, whether people get the vaccine or not. We'll need you to store the blood locally until independent auditors can verify them. In that way, it can't be claimed we switched them out at our lab."

"That sounds like a record-keeping nightmare."

Dave turned to Adrian whose World Bank team would oversee the coordination of data.

"We'll take care of the paperwork," Adrian said. "You only need to provide the people and the refrigerator."

"And the PR apparently." Hamara looked at Adrian from beneath furrowed brow.

"PR, but no spin," Adrian replied. "Just facts, Chief. I promise."

Hamara hugged Sara closer. He lifted his eyes toward Fr. Jim. Jim laid a hand on the chief's shoulder.

"Four months late," Hamara said. The men knew that Ketta, the chief's seven-year-old daughter, died from malaria in the summer. Sara leaned up and planted a kiss on her father's cheek before jumping off his lap. She ran after a group of children. Hamara's eyes followed her and then stopped as she passed a long ecru-colored building. "But not too late for Sara and the other children," he added and then pointed at the building. "That's our clinic."

More substantive than the other village buildings, the clinic's straight exterior walls had been plastered with mud over a wooden frame. Wood joists joined by wood shingles poked out of the front wall to cover a short plank deck at the entrance. On the side sat a large gas-powered generator, one of only two the village had.

"It's where Ketta and many others died," Hamara continued. "It's more of a quarantine center than a place of healing. We don't even have a nurse. We rely on outside medical people coming in every few months. It's not enough."

"I've offered you a solution for that," Adrian said. "You have a bona fide offer for the land from the Abo tribe. Sell it, pocket the money in the treasury for a rainy day, and move your tribe to the city."

Hamara ignored him.

"You don't have to listen, Chief. But your people will pay for your stubbornness. Many with their lives."

Dave flinched. He was blindsided by Adrian's agenda to get Hamara to sell the tribe's land. He fought back the temptation to blast the World Bank exec. He swallowed a deep breath followed by a drink of his iced tea. The ice cube had melted, the slight chill in the liquid still refreshing on this hot and muggy morning. "We're not here to discuss relocating the Lokoma," he said calmly to Adrian. "We're here about the vaccine and saving lives."

Activity about 20 yards behind Hamara caught Dave's attention. Among a large group of children, Jacob twirled Sara in circles while she tilted her head back, mouth wide open, giggling. The sound put him at ease, just as Liv's giggles always did.

Hamara followed Dave's line of sight. "Our most important resource," Hamara said. "But we lose one in five to disease before they're five years old."

"That's unacceptable in this day and age," Adrian said.

"It's God's will. But your technology is coming now. That's God's will, too. It's not his will to sell the land of our ancestors to another tribe. Instead, we need to find a way to make my people comfortable with the technology and let it help us."

"What if we get a PDNA in here early?" the priest suggested. "Let them touch it and play with it. Make it more toy than technology so that everyone can get comfortable with it."

"That would work," Dave said. "I have functional demo units in Colorado. We can ship you one with sampling kits."

"That would help," Hamara said.

Suddenly, a loud explosion shook the ground. Screams and shouting filled the air. All the men except Hamara dove to the dirt.

Seconds later, Dave looked up and saw Hamara running toward flames and billowing smoke on the edge of the village. Dave jumped to his feet and the others followed, trailing Hamara over a narrow path cut amidst the trees and brush. In less than a minute, they arrived at the site of the blast on a large plateau behind the village. There, a cassava crop and other vegetables grew in patches. The plateau had sourced food and income for the Lokoma for centuries. Now, shrapnel and smoke covered much of the crop, the leaves of many of the cassava plants burning as villagers raced in with buckets of water.

One heavyset villager approached Hamara. "We need to arm," he said. "When will you listen?"

Hamara walked toward the field, offering no response. He looked across the plateau to a distant scar of stripped land in the rainforest, land where the tribe had mined bauxite, the key ingredient in the manufacture of aluminum. The civil war had dried up the export business. The mine - and its income stream for the Lokoma - closed in the early days of the fighting when the bauxite processing companies pulled out of the country.

Hamara turned back toward the village, still saying nothing.

"It's a warning, Chief," Adrian called after him.

Hamara kept walking.

"You need to re-locate," Adrian continued. "The Abo offer is a fair deal."

Hamara spoke while looking straight ahead as he walked. "You've badgered me with this for months. The Abo do nothing out of the goodness of their heart. This is Lokoma land and they have no right to it."

"The Lokoma aren't safe here," Adrian explained. "The civil war may be over in Freetown and the cities, but bands of well-armed thieves and so-called rebels still roam the bush."

Fr. Jim spoke. "It's the Lokoma's home. Has been for centuries. You don't easily walk away from your roots."

"There are no easy choices, Father."

Hamara said nothing. Instead, he led the men back to a small circle of mud and thatch huts near the village center. The huts had dirt floors and single doorways covered with strung beads and shells. Reserved for food preparation, one hut had a large smokestack in its center. He pushed one set of beads aside.

"My parents' home," he said.

He walked seven yards and pushed aside another set of beads hanging in a doorway. "The home of Jacob's mother."

Ani, Jacob's mother, had her own one-room hut in the compound where she and Jacob lived. On the trip up, Adrian had explained to Dave and Evan that the village converted to Catholicism from its traditional tribal religion a few years after Dave's medical mission that brought the eyeglasses. At that time, Hamara had to choose only one wife since Christianity proscribed polygamy. Barren since giving birth to Jacob, Ani could not fulfill the need for a large family to farm and hunt. Mariama had already produced one daughter, making her the most viable choice for his only wife. A few months after the annulment, Mariama became pregnant with Sara. That left Ani, at 25, a divorced woman with a son and no prospects for marriage in the village. She taught Jacob to be angry about his father's choice.

Hamara moved to a third larger hut and pushed its beads aside as well. It was empty except for cooking utensils and rolled-up mats on the floor. Mosquito netting hung from the ceiling.

"My home," he said.

"You can have so much more," Adrian said.

"We have everything. And a man like you, living alone thousands of miles from any family or real friends, should appreciate that."

Adrian started to say more, but Hamara turned away from him to speak to Dave and Evan. "Bring us your machine and your vaccine," the Chief said. "That gives us hope. We welcome hope."

CHAPTER 9

Liv's Diary Entry
October 16, 2:50 a.m. Mountain Time

Sleep's not happening tonight. I have no clue how I'll get up for school in less than four hours.

The stalker is real. I am not crazy.

Two nights since he texted. Every noise wakes me. Doesn't help that it's windy. I wish Mom believed me. I wish it was the medication, too, but I don't believe that.

I tried to sit with Mom and talk to her. She wanted to watch TV instead. And lecture me about keeping a knife. Dad's our best protection and she won't let him come home.

School's probably not helping me sleep either. Today was horrible beyond words. Lauren said a lot of things about Emily at lunch. She thinks she's funny, but Lauren's not funny. I could see Emily was upset and I couldn't not defend her. (Mrs. Woodruff would mark me down for a double negative on that one.)

My mistake. Lauren turned on me instead, saying I was a fat a__. Which I'm definitely not. She was laughing like it was a big joke. Hahaha. Then Emily joined in. After I defended her! That made me mad. I didn't show it. I just laughed and tried to change the subject. But it was everything I could do to keep from crying. I'm probably overly sensitive from hormones or the drugs. I texted Chelsea the details from class later. She told me I was definitely NOT in the wrong. Nice to have a good friend I can count on.

Chels told me her parents got her a new iPod nano. A pink one. #coolparents. My mom won't let me get an iPod because she's worried about money. So I listen on a two year old smartphone that doesn't even begin to hold all my music and loses its place when I'm texting. Dad will get either an iPod or a new phone for me – if I ever see him again. I said that to Mom. Not a good move. She went ballistic.

At least, she doesn't ask me about my sex life anymore. No matter what she wants to think, I did not bring this on myself. I only wish I had some kind of sex life. I'd settle for someone who knew how to kiss. But I'd probably make him sick like me.

Mom still won't let Dad see me. It's like I'm some prize he has to earn. He needs to be home, at least to protect us. A stalker's not about to mess with my Dad. She's punishing him because he never had time for me before. He used to really hurt my feelings, but I think Mom hurts me more these days. I really want to see him, even for only a little bit. When she told me he's in West Africa I whispered a prayer right away. That's a seriously scary part of the world with street gangs, civil wars, malaria and Ebola.

I'll sign off for tonight. I have way too much homework PLUS I'm very, very tired. I'm taking all my pills when I'm supposed to, even if Mom and the doctor think they make me a whack-job. I'm good just as long as my HIV doesn't build resistance again. That would suck since there are only so many meds you can take for this. I still seem to get more and more exhausted every day. Part of it's probably the effect of the pills. Doc Resnick says they're pretty strong. But I also have no doubt that part of it is the stress of Dad being gone. That's definitely one big reason Mom acts so mad all the time. It's because she still loves him. I caught her crying. I didn't tell her how I cry myself to sleep most nights - when I can sleep. It's already hard enough for her.

CHAPTER 10

Boulder, Colorado: Health Club
October 16, 6:08 a.m. Mountain Time

Claire McQuaid put her coffee down on the top shelf of the locker and checked her phone for the time. 6:08 a.m. She wanted to be at her office by 7:15 to get an update on Dave Clement's progress in Lagos. Plenty of time, she thought. She looked around the locker room to make sure no one else remained at this early hour. Taking a deep breath, she quickly pulled her workout tee shirt over her head and stuffed it in her locker. Next she stepped out of her sweat pants and thong. In the mirror across the room, she caught a glimpse of herself. She wanted to believe that she felt nothing but determination when she saw herself naked, accustomed to the body scars that drew stares and even an occasional gasp when others saw them. As always, she did not want to deal with any of that this morning. She wrapped a robe around herself and headed to the steam room. She turned the steam to the highest setting and disappeared into the thick mist, inhaling the eucalyptus. She draped a towel on one of the tile steps. Shedding the robe, she lay down.

The room's anonymity provided sanctuary and liberation for her. No one could see her clearly. No one knew her. And she liked her nakedness in here. She could run her hands over her hot, wet skin and feel like any other woman, enjoying the touch, even if it was her own. It had been rare that a man had touched her. There had been a few that seemed to accept her as she was, but she had rejected them. She could not tolerate acceptance of her deformities.

One particularly gorgeous man had even claimed a deep love for her saying he loved her scars because they were part of her. Her rage in response surprised even her. The relationship sputtered on for a few months after that, but ultimately died. Accepting her scars meant accepting their origins. Claire could not allow that, not until she finished her work, a complex matrix of carefully synchronized elements that only she could execute.

She closed her eyes and tried to concentrate on the wet heat, working to keep memories and obsession from overwhelming her thoughts. She knew that would begin again when she left the gym. For now, she needed to find a little balance, if only for a few minutes.

She coaxed her fingertips slowly and lightly along the sides of her abdomen and then down the outside of her thighs. It felt comforting. As one hand slid between her thighs, the other glided back to her chest, caressing her disfigurement. There she felt the searing flames again. In an instant, the emptiness returned, the loneliness that started when they ripped her mother and baby sister from her life. "Go away," she mumbled. "Dammit. Go away."

Tears, undetectable in the wet steam room, dripped down the sides of her face.

CHAPTER 11

Boulder, Colorado, Aldrich Institute Headquarters
October 16, 8:30 am Mountain Time (MT)

Two hours later, Claire perused e-mail on her phone while the presenter droned on in the darkened conference room. The marketing detail interested her, but she had already reviewed the presentation. This was for the benefit of her research and development managers.

She tapped on a message from Dave Clement that told her that the meetings in Sierra Leone had gone well. Good news. Conger, Guerra, and the Leoneans had all played well together. The Aldrich and Dave's company, Prodeus, could deliver malaria vaccine and PDNAs as soon as Thanksgiving. An aggressive schedule, but do-able if she kept the pressure on everyone. Jennifer would keep an eye on Dave Clement and the Prodeus side of things for her. She still did not have the man in full control, but Claire knew Jenn would get him there. The dirty tricks manual had by no means been exhausted.

An alert box appeared in the middle of her phone. With her index finger, she tapped the "view" option on the screen. News of the latest attack scrolled across the bottom. She had set an app to alert her to any headline that included the words terror, bomb, attack, and other similar keywords.

As she read the latest headline, her cheeks reddened. She stood, abruptly excusing herself from the meeting. Hardly breathing, her two-inch heels clicked double-time down the corridor, the peace from her early morning visit to the gym evaporating quickly. She heard someone coming and accelerated her pace, turning sharply into her office in front of two passing assistants working up the nerve to say hello.

She closed the door behind her, the lock clicking beneath her thumb. Her third floor corner office had no internal windows, only windows to the outside. Looking out on Boulder's sunlit flatirons, she recalled a recurring nightmare. In it, the long cliffs of the flatirons crumbled before her eyes, sliding down the mountainside into the University of Colorado campus. She stood on the cobblestones in the middle of Pearl Street Mall as a great cloud of pitch-black dust overwhelmed her and everything else in sight. In the end, she found herself surrounded by impenetrable darkness, gasping for breath.

Now seated behind her desk, she went to the news site sourcing the story and quickly found the headline she sought: "Terror strikes Paris-area superstore; 17 dead."

Downloading the news report, she extracted the video showing the bombed-out front entrance of the store, a French variation of Wal-Mart with at least twice the square footage. She clipped shots of severed limbs and one headless body, observing that the French media more willingly exposed gruesome details than Americans did.

She pasted the 15 seconds of edited video to a longer video she had been nurturing. Putting on a set of headphones, she clicked the play button with the mouse. The main video started. For what may have been the thousandth time, she watched a commercial airliner fly into the World Trade Center in lower Manhattan, an explosion of flame bursting out the other side of the building. She watched clinically as people tumbled through the air from over one hundred stories up. On her headphones, she heard the rumble and then the amplified roar as each building collapsed. Over the years, she found her emotions had grown more and more numb when viewing the montage of havoc that flashed across the screen. Part of her worried that she had become accustomed to the ruthless destruction.

On the screen, she saw Rwandans and Leoneans howl as machete wielding boys chopped off their limbs; she watched women beheaded in a stadium in Kabul. Before her eyes, the Oklahoma City federal building once again poured in pieces into the street. And the rubble of department store entryways piled high on innocent shoppers of all sizes, races, and genders – eight minutes of carnage, eight minutes that once tore away at her heart now immunized it to the brutal task ahead. The video reminded her not to lose focus.

Underlying the noise of bombs exploding and buildings collapsing, the 1812 overture played on her headphones. Then the volume of the sounds grew quieter as her late father's voice came on. "There are no limits to the love we have for one another. No boundaries of time and space. Nothing that can be killed by the hateful. We must stop this madness. It has no limits and infects the world like a cancer. In the name of all that have gone before us, we must eradicate this plague…"

The music came up again, the loud explosions of cannon at the end of the overture acting as counterpoint to scenes flashing by on the computer screen, including shots of people missing limbs or otherwise horribly scarred. Claire's face grew placid, her lips set. She inhaled a deep breath remembering her own searing pain.

As the video ended, she looked up at the ornate ceiling tiles in her office. She did not feel so alone after watching the video. In some unexplained way, it made her feel peaceful. Then, after a moment, a small leak of emotion: a single tear dribbled down her cheek.

She turned her chair to face the Boulder flatirons. She saw shadows of great fluffy clouds drifting over the massive layers of wedge-shaped rock in the mid-afternoon sun, the melting snow from a few days earlier still dotting crevices like drippings from a painter's brush. Slowly, she doubled over as the familiar deep ache in the center of her belly throbbed and grew in agonizing intensity. Tears finally welled up in her eyes again as memory attacked her from within.

> *...She saw nothing, felt nothing. Her father's voice called out to them, but she couldn't answer.*

CHAPTER 12

Freetown, Sierra Leone; Kenya Airways Flight
October 16, 6:05 pm GMT

His eyes flapped open, sweat dribbling down his neck. The plane's engines roared as it accelerated down the runway, almost imperceptibly lifting off the concrete. He had nodded off while they waited on the steaming tarmac in Freetown. As usual, he did not remember his dream, but he vaguely recalled being with Liv and Mel. He felt consumed with a sense of danger that still lingered after he woke. He wanted to call them, but that would not be possible for almost three hours as the plane soared east over West Africa bound for a Delta connection in Accra, Ghana.

Gazing through the scratches and fog on the window beside his seat, he saw sky-blue, crystal clear water and long rows of white foam, spaced perhaps thirty yards apart, rolling onto a sandy shore lined with palms. A canopy of lush, green jungle cascaded down the coastline's steep hills to meet the sand. In the distance, he could see the whitewashed buildings of Freetown casting long shadows from beneath their red tile roofs in the setting sun. As the plane maneuvered into its flight path, the illusion created by distance faded; he now saw big shantytowns on the outskirts of the city and bombed-out buildings within it. It looked like a beautiful jewel that someone had attacked with a giant ice pick.

As the plane reached a cruising altitude of 38,000 feet, he closed his eyes and envisioned waves breaking on a shore, but on the couple of occasions when that meditation drifted into sleep, trays clattering in the cabin or turbulent air jarred him back into wide-eyed wakefulness.

Nagging anxiety poked at his stomach throughout the trip. His mind drifted obsessively into stressful areas, making the sleep effort even more difficult. The portable DNA analyzer, a four-year obsession, fought for mindshare with guilt about his family. Even with the help of Fr. Jim and Adrian Guerra's World Bank, along with Evan Conger's WHO inroads in Sierra Leone, deployment would be challenging. The Leonean government viewed the program as a step toward healing not only malaria but also the emotional wounds that still ravaged the country long after the final combat truce. Not all the chiefs and religious leaders agreed. Superstition, suspicion, and dissatisfaction with the economic direction of the tenuous peace threatened to fuel further conflict. To facilitate a more permanent peace in the region, Conger had taken an earlier flight to New York; there, he would meet with Pamela Thatcher, probably the single-most politically influential investment banker in the US, to affirm the funding path and discuss ongoing diplomatic and nation-building efforts.

Dave also pondered the potential dangers associated with the few rebel bands that remained. Isolation of the threatened areas could minimize the danger, but the project needed good advice in-country to determine how best to do that. Even after the truce, people had been kidnapped or murdered randomly in and around the capital itself. Dave did not want any of his team members added to those statistics.

Still, something far more personal drove his anxiety. For the first time, he would be returning from an international trip without Liv and Mel waiting for him, without their hugs and touch reassuring him.

He re-lived the moment Liv had emerged from the womb 15 years earlier. He had wondered why God had rewarded him.

Cradling the newborn in his arms, he pondered her, felt her emotionally. He recognized her as pure and untouched by the world she had just entered. He studied his tiny new daughter, his thoughts folding into the eddy that swirled from her clear blue eyes, spinning the reflection of surgical lights into the luminous aura of ten thousand angels. As he succumbed to the moment, a unique peace saturated his mind and body; a numbness – like a spiritual lobotomy – calmed the unfolding pleats of stress on his forehead.

In the vortex over his tiny daughter, his universe found a new center.

As he held her in his arms, his surgical mask still on for her protection, Liv blinked back the brightness. Soft, pink skin still glistened from the fluids that had nurtured her for nine months. Her eyes adjusting, she gazed curiously at Dave.

In that moment, he knew no self-awareness, connecting on a level he had never before experienced. His love for Mel had never been fuller. When the nurse gently nudged Liv from his arms, he kissed Mel delicately on the lips, the softness drawing them together. He stroked her hair and recounted her virtues. He babbled about what a beautiful baby she made.

She told him to shut up. Then kissed him back.

Now, fifteen years later, as his flight bounced through turbulence over the rolling forests of southern Guinea, he wondered if his sins, more recently ingratitude manifested as inattention and self-centeredness, had come back to square things. And he could not ignore the sixth sense that an even more sinister Karma yet lay in wait.

CHAPTER 13

Cameron Pass, Aldrich Mountain Lab
October 16, 1:15 p.m. MDT

Standing between the pale-green concrete block walls in the white fluorescent-lit hallway, Sheila Stratemeier knocked on the door. She heard the faint whir of a small motor as the tiny camera over the door focused on her. A hum sounded indicating the lock's release. Sheila turned the knob and entered, closing the door behind her as Eldridge always insisted.

The room made her hair stand on end. Eldridge Perry never had any lights on, preferring to work by the light of the monitor with a miniscule USB powered lamp lighting the keyboard.

With Eldridge's dark skin and a penchant for wearing black shirts, Sheila detected only the slightly phosphorescent glow of his eyes until her own eyes adjusted to the dark.

No guest chairs existed in the office, so Sheila carried on her discussion while standing. "I swear you're some kind of mole, Eldridge."

"Keeps me focused. No external stimulants to distract me. Except for you at the moment. Is there some reason this couldn't wait for our staff meeting?"

"This isn't the kind of discussion we should have in front of the rest of the team."

"Why's that?" His eyes drifted backward in the room, indicating he had tilted his chair. Sheila thought she detected a letter opener in his hands.

"Because you might view a public discussion of it as undermining you and Claire." Sheila respected Claire McQuaid. Claire had mentored her since Sheila's arrival seven years ago. She and Jennifer Winter, hired within weeks of one another, had been the first women other than McQuaid recruited into the Institute's bio-engineering ranks.

"That's thoughtful," Eldridge said.

"I thought so."

"This isn't about your damned priorities again, is it?"

"It is."

"You're wasting my time. I thought Claire told you the same thing."

The room suddenly darkened even more as the monitor entered its dark sleep mode. Sheila's head spun, the change disorienting her.

"Nice effect, isn't it?" Eldridge said.

"You're definitely not the norm, boss."

"So why would you expect me to follow the norm in rolling out our plans in West Africa?"

"What harm does it do to finish human testing of CEM15-D first? It's insane to deploy Vif-D without it."

Sheila's team had synthesized CEM15-D and Vif-D to replace the cellular proteins CEM15 and Vif in the human body. The two proteins played different roles in the body's war with HIV and AIDS. CEM15 protected the body against HIV. Vif, short for Viral Infectivity Factor, fought against CEM15, disrupting CEM15's antiviral activity in the body, breaking down the immune system for takeover by HIV. This breakdown ultimately led to AIDS and death over a period of many years.

Sheila's synthetic "D" versions, however, completely changed the rules of cellular war. Vif-D alone wiped out CEM15, bringing about sero-conversion of HIV to AIDS in weeks, resulting in death within months. But when Sheila's team then mutated CEM15 to CEM-15D, synthetic CEM15-D wiped out Vif-D almost overnight, resulting in the first known cure for AIDS. So the secret was to give HIV victims a much more lethal HIV virus that could be eradicated by CEM15-D, replacing the slow moving HIV that continued to elude a cure.

Eldridge's voice deepened as he became more intractable. "We can and we will deploy Vif-D."

"But when CEM15-D is ready. Not now. Vif-D by itself kills. Always. And in a matter of months."

"We know what we're doing, Sheila."

"You're risking thousands of lives, maybe tens of thousands."

"Maybe hundreds of thousands," he countered.

"Dear God, Eldridge. We have no right to do this. If you just wait for my team to finish CEM15-D, we have a chance to save most of those people. Once we give them the malaria vaccine with the Vif-D Trojan horse inside, they'll have less than four months to live. If we can't get CEM15-D to them in that time, we're looking at mass casualties."

"So finish CEM15-D."

"You know as well as I do that we need a lot more time to get it right."

"Listen, Sheila. The people you're worried about are already dead. In sub-Saharan Africa, AIDS is almost a certain death sentence. There's no hope. Even if the CEM15-D process were ready to roll out now, you still need to get the antibodies from those with the new HIV in order to finish it."

"We planned for that."

"You did. We didn't. Trust that we know what we're doing. There's a bigger picture here."

"I can't imagine what bigger picture would justify this."

"See. That's the problem with our world today, Sheila. People aren't willing to make the hard decisions. Well, the fact is, sacrifices need to be made to bring about great breakthroughs. Our program may cause some people with HIV to die sooner than they might have otherwise. But also because of us and because of the sacrifice of these people, their survivors will beat AIDS. The scourge will be stopped."

"This is wrong, Eldridge. And you know it."

"AIDS is the culprit here. AIDS raised the stakes. Not us. We have to think about future generations and the well-being of the hundreds of millions not yet infected. Even if the price ends up being as high as a few million early deaths around the world, that number will seem trivial in a decade if we don't act now."

Sheila tried to see his face. Was there a glimmer of sarcasm? Did he mean everything he said? "I'm not going to let this happen, Eldridge."

"It will happen. With or without you."

"Then do it without me."

"There's only one way you get out of here before this project is done," he said. "Feet first."

"Is that a threat?"

"I have work to do."

"I asked you if that's a threat."

Eldridge remained silent for the next several minutes. Hopelessness gnawing at her, Sheila finally left the office angry – and afraid.

CHAPTER 14

Liv's Diary
October 17, 6:50 a.m. Mountain Time

Yay! Dad's back in the USA. He left a phone message from the Atlanta airport. He's going to be back in Colorado later this morning.

We were here when he called at 6:30 this morning, but Mom wouldn't let me pick up. She was dressed in her biking gear, ready to hit the road for her morning workout in the dark. She's a fanatic. The sun won't even be up until after 7.

When I walked out into the hallway, she told me to go back to sleep. She doesn't realize that I wake up every morning when I hear her leaving the house for her bike roadwork. Sometimes I get back to sleep; mostly I don't.

I don't believe her when she says she's not mad at him anymore. To be real, if she wasn't mad, she'd let him move back in. She says she'll let him move back in when he gets his priorities straight.

I think it's me. He can't deal with it. He doesn't want to. Not to feel sorry for myself, but I know I'm a huge disappointment, just a sick, irritating teenager. And Chelsea called me bitchy yesterday. She wasn't trying to be funny. And she's my oldest friend. So it hurts.

But Mom's the bitchy one lately, not me, although I definitely can be that way. The way Mom acts may be exactly why Dad spent all his time at work. There are way too many days when I can understand that. I've thought about spending more time out of the house, but I know that Mom's bitchy because of me and my little 'problem'. It's not just self-pity to think the two of them might be happier and a whole lot better off without me. I'm the person with the problem and I'm sick of dealing with it. I can only imagine how they feel.

So I skipped a dose last night. And I didn't say any prayers. Even God's sick of me. He's proven that. Maybe I'm sick of Him, too.

CHAPTER 15

Lokoma Village
October 17, 3:30 p.m. Greenwich Mean Time

Hamara Karanja squatted beside Sara. She lay sweating profusely on a sleep mat spread on the hard dirt floor. Light creeping through the thatch overhead streaked Sara's five-year-old frame with splotches of brightness. Her father's sinewed hand stroked her hair and temples. Her skin felt soft, smooth and frighteningly hot to his touch.

"Papa," she whispered, her wide eyes gazing at his silhouette in the dim hut. "I don't want to be sick anymore."

He reached for a clear, plastic bottle of warm water beside him. "Drink this, Sara," he encouraged as he placed the spout to her lips.

"Nooo," she moaned.

"Dear, you need to. We have to keep water in you or you could get sicker."

"Papa, I don't think I can get sicker."

"It will help make you better."

Conceding, she pursed her lips to receive the water. Hamara tilted the bottle slightly to allow the water to dribble over her lips and tongue. He had sent Jacob for ice at the community room and wondered why he was not back yet.

"How's that?" he asked his daughter.

"Mmmm," she groaned. "I think I have to go to the bathroom again."

"Are you sure?"

In the dimness, he could see her shake her head affirmatively. He put an arm under her shoulder and helped her up. The amulet strung around her neck caught on the mat. He disdainfully yanked it free; Mariama had insisted Sara wear it. She argued that it couldn't hurt. Many of the Lokoma thought the cowry-shell amulet could draw the fever out of a body. Hamara did not. Were it a contagion like Ebola, the amulet would, in fact, provide a means to spread the disease. Hamara briefly thanked God that it was not Ebola, a virus with a truly hopeless prognosis for its victims.

Sara tried to wobble to her feet, but Hamara put another arm under her knees and lifted her into the air. He carried her out the door of the hut, leaning forward over her, trying to cast the shadow of his head and shoulders on her. In this way, he hoped to protect her eyes from the bright sunlight.

He walked ten yards to the common latrine. The stench always peaked at this time of day, the heat bringing the odors to life. He carried her inside and set her down on the small wooden commode. As soon as she settled, she let out a small howl. He heard the gushing of her bowels pouring into the stagnant water below. He steeled himself against the smell and kept a gentle hand on her shoulder as she shivered from weakness and fever.

Her little body had grown gaunt in just the last 36 hours, her cheekbones and jaw over-pronounced as the fat stores and water that once puffed her face had now diminished to dangerously low levels. Through eye sockets deepened by this depletion, enormous brown eyes, glistening with tears, looked up at Hamara. She inhaled a deep swallow of the pungent air and squeezed out a grateful smile as her head bobbed weakly on her small, frail neck. Her face creased again into pain. She tucked her chin into her chest and bent forward as more drained into the pit.

He had no quinine sulphate tablets for her. He had texted Fr. Jim earlier in the day, and Jim promised to bring some up in the morning. As many times as he had seen children with malaria, Hamara remained stunned at how quickly the disease tore a child down, especially his child.

He knew how they might treat her differently in the west. Western hospitals hooked people to intravenous fluids as soon as possible to fight dehydration and fever. Today, at the un-staffed clinic, Hamara had asked one of the elders how they could do the same.

"We have no way to do this, Pa," village council member Musa said, using the term of respect reserved for chiefs and diviners. "The fluids would have to be both sterile and refrigerated. And we would need the intravenous equipment. Plus a way to mix the drugs. We have none of that."

The chief stared through Musa as though he could force a better answer.

"There's Freetown," Musa suggested. "They have the equipment at the hospital there."

"Fr. Jim will have quinine tablets for her tomorrow." Hamara did not want to think of relying on Freetown.

When he told Mariama they would wait for the quinine tablets, she reacted. "That's too long. We should take her to Freetown now."

"By the time we leave, it will be dark. Sara is at greater risk on the road with bandits at that hour than she is if she waits for the drug."

"Maboro is needed then," Mariama said. "Something on which we can rely."

"It defies science," he said.

"Science defies generations of learning by our ancestors. The ancestors remain around us watching, protecting us from the devils that fill the forest. Trying to bring us back to who we once were."

"And who were we?"

"A proud, ancient tribe with spirits that kept us well – as long as we remained faithful to our ancestors."

"They did not save Ketta."

"Perhaps, Pa, the spirit world needed her. Perhaps she even left to watch over us."

He wanted to tell her that she could not mean that, but he knew she clung to hope with thoughts like this. Those thoughts provided no comfort to him, however. As a chief, he needed to rise above simple answers and deal with the messiness of real life.

Still, he could not help but long to feel his oldest little girl in his arms again, squeezing her close and finding a way to keep her safe.

And now he found himself standing in the bathroom watching another daughter quivering with fever and deteriorating. He could not allow her to continue to suffer. He could not risk losing her, too.

CHAPTER 16

Loveland, Colorado; Dave Clement's Office at Prodeus, Inc.
October 18, 7:15 a.m.

As the sun peeked over the horizon on the eastern plains, rivers of light in shades of pink, yellow and purple flowed over the ridges and crevices on the western mountains of northern Colorado's Front Range, pushing night's last shadows down into the foothills below. Atop the gray rocky slopes of Longs Peak, the new season's first snow glistened silver-white against a backdrop of brilliant blue sky. Just below the 14,000 foot plus crest, a white glacier sliced through the ancient rock, steadily shrinking as each new carbon-burning year passed.

In the grassy field between Dave's office and the mountains, a chestnut stallion awoke, running back and forth, dawn's golden glow on its withers. Sipping coffee, Dave thought this had to be one of the few places on earth compelling one to look west at dawn.

No one else had yet arrived this morning. Dave liked being here alone and free of interruptions. Once the parking lot started filling, people inevitably appeared at his door with questions or chit-chat. He had experimented with keeping his door closed, but found he preferred the interaction. Plus it made him less of a mystery to his people, helping to keep them empowered and self-motivated. And he liked the conversation, liked the people. He thought of them as a cross between family and friends, sometimes his only friends.

Dave's eyes passed slowly over the framed pictures of Liv on his credenza. A laughing nine month old pulling up on her playpen, diaper pooching out the back. A three-year-old, face full of innocence and adoration for her Daddy. An eight year old with her Daddy at a pumpkin farm, orange and red leaves all over the ground, bright grins and red cheeks on their faces.

Then, Mel's picture – the two of them, smiling into a camera held by a good Samaritan on the beach in Captiva, both of them much younger, Dave much slimmer, Mel's face unlined and betraying naiveté, now long faded.

He remembered the demand of the CEO at Genofot, the insistence that he ignore the embellishments in the FDA filing.

"What the hell's wrong with you, Dave?" the CEO had said. "The drug changes lives."

"It cures baldness, Fred. And it diminishes penile functionality in 15% of the test group."

"We don't know that."

"We have evidence and we should disclose it."

"Dave, you don't understand the science. You're a partnership guy. And the best in the business, but you don't understand the science. We have no way of knowing for certain what the performance of these men was like before the drug. They're older men. Their cocks go soft. It's mother nature. Why should our drug take the rap for that?"

"We need to test for it, Fred."

"Why does this matter so much to you? You're our key guy with UNESCO on our anti-malarials and anti-retrovirals. Don't let a baldness drug screw up your career."

"Are you threatening me?"

"Face it, Dave. Who the hell wants a guy around who undermines the company?"

"Here's what worries me. If you're willing to lie to the FDA on something as trivial as a baldness drug, what are you willing to do to get a leg up on something as critical as anti-retrovirals and anti-malarials?"

"Baldness drug's worth a lot more money. Does that answer your question? Vanity trumps life and death every time when it comes to revenue."

In a careless moment, Dave whispered his concerns about Genofot's ethics to a friend in UNESCO. As a result, Genofot lost an opportunity to do a pilot program. And Fred fired Dave summarily. For almost four years, Dave went without being hired by a pharmaceutical company. Instead, he relied on short consulting contracts with UNESCO and the World Health Organization. While be built a powerful reputation for pulling people and programs together in that community, there were many lengthy gaps between contracts when he brought home no income. The financial stress mounted during those four years. And his relationship with Mel lost some of its luster as she often found herself the only breadwinner with family overhead that required two.

So when Evan Conger, who had contracted with him for WHO, referred him for the slot at Prodeus, his life finally got back on track. Since arriving, he had worked very hard to make Prodeus successful, re-establishing his reputation as the top partnership development exec in the industry, a very important skill to both Prodeus and the Aldrich. He was relentless with himself on the time and effort he expended. He needed the job to work for the benefit of his family, particularly now with Liv's HIV. But his obsession with the work also undermined his family. Some days the path to a win seemed very unclear.

As his reverie drifted from melancholy into frustration, he turned back to his work. With the flourish of a concert pianist, he poised his hands over the keyboard. Blowing the air out of his lungs, he pushed his thoughts into the background and began scrolling through the distraction of his e-mail.

Claire McQuaid wanted an update on his trip. He had written a trip report during the leg from Accra to Atlanta. He would e-mail that to her after reading it through one more time. He would set up a lunch meeting, too – probably near her office in Boulder because he liked the restaurants in Boulder – but not until he knew the status of the PDNA. That update would come at his nine o'clock staff meeting.

He opened the file "Trip Report West Africa" On his computer. After re-reading it and making some minor modifications, he attached it to an e-mail for McQuaid and a handful of the members of his own team.

Further perusing e-mail, he clicked on the daily update from The Body, a site that specialized in information on HIV. He digested every article, clicking the links in search of meaningful tidbits. The material seemed well-worn to him by now, but every now and then a new insight cropped up. There had to be some other way to contract it. He knew she had never had a blood transfusion. And he believed Liv's claim that she had no history of sexual activity. At least, he wanted to believe it.

He checked the Amazon cloud repository he and Sheila had set up to keep others from accessing their communications. Nothing new from her. He uploaded a quick note to her that simply said: "Any progress?"

He heard noises in the hall as other people arrived. He should have done the HIV homework first; the trip report could have been done with people in the building. Through his door, he saw one of the firmware engineers disappear into the cubicles that filled most of the second floor. Dave still had time.

He clicked a hopeful link on The Body site. No new information. No magic pill to make HIV go away. And no magic pill to make the last six months go away.

A tapping on his office door caused Dave to look up to see a smiling Jennifer standing in the doorway.

"G'morning, boss," she said, dropping into a chair.

In keeping with the company's casual style, Jennifer wore jeans and an unbuttoned aqua polo with the Prodeus logo embroidered on the upper-left side, factory fashion only tolerable within the company walls. Many of the engineers wore their company knits about town when not working. Hence the word "geek," according to Jennifer. She once told Dave that she changed into a spare blouse in her car as soon as she hit the parking lot at the end of the day.

In spite of the work attire, Jennifer's red hair bobbed on her shoulders at a cost of about $200 per month at a hairdresser 40 minutes away in Boulder. The creases of the shirt were sharp, its collar up and its buttons undone, framing a turquoise-and-silver neck chain she found on a long weekend in Santa Fe. The jeans showed crease down to her two-inch heels, walking shoes in Jennifer's world.

Dave knew she had studied him intensely since she had started working for him. His assistant, Ann, called it a weird obsession.

"Set jaw. Faraway look. A little sadness," Jennifer said Sherlock Holmes-like as she eased herself into one of the chairs. "Mel?"

Dave shrugged. Her fascination with him made him ill at ease.

"She let you see Liv yet?" Jennifer continued. She gazed at him with wet green eyes. She leaned across the desk, her cleavage peeking out from under the dangling Anasazi turquoise neck chain.

She laid a hand flat on the desk, extended for his hand should he get the hint - which he did and which he ignored.

"Not yet," he responded politely while glancing at the computer monitor. "What's up?"

She withdrew her hand. "I'm over here, Dave."

He turned back to her. "Sorry. Lots going on."

"I'm concerned for you. You're already under a lot of stress at work. You don't need any more at home..."

He flashed a glare at her. Jennifer paused and sat back, crossing her legs and wrapping her hands around her knee.

"So how was the heart of darkness?" she asked.

Dave swiveled the monitor out of the way. She'd hit his hot button. "It's not your place to judge my wife. I love her very much. If I step back from the situation, her frustration's easy to understand. I've been an absentee father. When I was home, I either talked about work or fell asleep in front of the TV. Very much a one-dimensional experience."

Jennifer offered a weak smile, more sympathetic than defensive. "By heart of darkness, I meant Africa," she said.

He knitted his brow.

"Joseph Conrad," she explained. "The novel?"

His felt his face flush hot with embarrassment. "Of course," he said as he brushed a hand over his forehead.

"I don't know about Mel. And I agree it's none of my business. But I think you need a Liv fix."

Dave grunted, a small grin forming.

"Maybe you could figure out where she goes after school and run into her," she said

"Stalk her?"

"It's not stalking when you're the dad. I wish my father had cared enough to stalk me."

Dave smiled. "She probably still hangs out at the mall after volleyball practice. Unless she's at the rock gym. That's her latest thing."

"That sounds like fun."

"Maybe. I'm not sure I understand the passion for climbing walls."

"Oh, I do. Remember the vacation week I took in March? I spent it on an Outward Bound trip to Joshua Tree. Great climbing there. It gets in your blood."

"Dangling from a rope on a cliff sounds like a death wish."

"Zest for life."

"Then I guess you and Liv must love life."

"Maybe you should try it," she offered. "I'll bet that would get her attention. I can show you the ropes. Literally."

He knew that would not be a good move. "No, thanks," he said. Pausing for a deep breath, he changed the subject. "Sierra Leone. Interesting visit. Makes you really appreciate what we have here.

Jennifer hesitated. He waited for her to press more about personal issues. Instead, she picked up a yellow pad and started taking notes. Her scent floated across the desk. A mix of hair conditioner and perfume. He wondered if she did it on purpose. Mel, never a fan of Jennifer, told him she probably spent hours in cosmetic departments figuring out the right chemistry for her body and her objectives. She would not waste that effort by selecting hair products that undermined the effect.

Pen poised, she waited for the series of action items he normally fired off. She looked up at him. Her green eyes shimmered.

"Nigeria is off the page for now," he continued. "I ended up right in the middle of a mortar attack in Lagos. They're killing kids. Little kids. It's just random. And some of the imams in the north continue to insist that the polio vaccine is both a Trojan horse for HIV and some kind of infertility drug the West is using to destroy them."

"Sounds hopeless."

"Not hopeless, but not a good place to pilot the PDNA. They'd probably smash them with sledgehammers."

"So we deploy in Sierra Leone. Sounds like the war's over."

"That's what they say. But we had mortars and small arms fire within hearing distance at Lokoma."

"Scary."

"The locals have adapted. We can't do anything about bombs and bullets, but we can get a PDNA to Lokoma."

"I got your e-mail. We're putting one through test today. It should go out tomorrow with the sampling kits. Day after at the latest."

"Thanks. So what am I going to see in staff this morning?"

"Good news mostly. The Aldrich sent us a fresh firmware update right after you left this time. We've only encountered minor issues in test so far. It looks like we're going to hit schedule."

"How's the lab?"

"Middleton's whining as usual."

Dave laughed a little. "He's an engineering VP. Comes with the territory. What's the problem now?"

"Same old. Brian wants the Aldrich to drop its drawers and show us the firmware source code."

"He's got a point, Jenn."

"Not going to happen, boss. McQuaid won't budge."

Dave sat back and steepled his fingers. He struggled to keep his eyes away from the smooth skin that formed the cleavage emerging between the undone buttons of her shirt.

Normally, the compulsion did not hit him this strongly, but two months of sleeping alone seemed to be taking its toll on his libido. He had never strayed on Mel and he had always been very careful about his interactions with women at work, even in his single years. But after years of growing accustomed to having a woman in bed beside him, living alone had left some needs unaddressed.

He felt stirrings he did not want. Jennifer wet her lips with her tongue and pushed her hair back behind her ears. She seemed to know exactly what she was doing. Dave's eyes hovered on her for an instant more before he quickly shifted his glance up to where Jennifer's eyes fixed on his.

"I understand Claire's concern," he said. "It's the family jewels, but Middleton has a point, too. We can't know if the test output is valid if we can't probe the firmware."

"Probing might be appropriate," she said. She smiled at him while pausing for several very long, uncomfortable seconds. Dave could not think of a response.

"But not for the Aldrich firmware," she finally added. "That's why we're in a joint venture. The Aldrich owns that one. We have to trust them."

"Have they sent their in-house test data to us?"

"They have. Middleton hasn't even looked at it yet."

"When did it get here?"

"Three days ago."

"Give the guy a break, Jenn. Three days isn't a long time. He has to run the lab."

"I just thought he'd be all over this one."

"Maybe he has more confidence in the Aldrich than he lets on."

Jennifer ran a hand back through her hair, completely exposing the pink creamy skin of her neck. Dave's eyes followed the movement. Her eyes flashed at him knowingly as she caught the direction of his glance. "You can look," she said.

He looked back at the computer screen instead, his lips pursed.

"So did you see Evan Conger?" she asked after another long pause.

Dave licked his dry lips before speaking. "We traveled together in Sierra

Leone. He knows his way around over there. And they respect him."

"He's brilliant, isn't he?"

"He knows his business."

"I worked under him at the Aldrich for two years before he went to Washington."

Dave hoped she did not intend a double meaning. "Did you have direct contact with him?" he asked.

"Not like I've had with you. There were a couple layers between us."

"Well, he's absolutely critical to deploying the malaria vaccine. The village-level leaders trust him. We should be able to avoid replicating the Nigerian situation."

Dave gathered a handful of loose papers on his desk and tapped them together into a neat pile.

"I have calls to make," he said.

...

Jennifer left Dave's office and went to the break area to make herself a cup of hot tea.

She thought she finally had Dave's intimate attention after months of trying. She thought about telling Dave she enjoyed having direct contact with him, that she wanted more. Too fast, she thought. He could spook and there was too much at stake. She thought of the second chin just starting on him; she remembered the little bit of excess pushing at his belt.

You do what you have to do, she told herself.

CHAPTER 17

Freetown Peninsula, Lokoma Road
October 18, 2:50 pm GMT

The old pick-up bounced through muddy ruts that inevitably filled the road by this stage of the rainy season. Fr. Jim peered over the steering wheel and through the film of smeared earth and bug splatter on the windshield. That mess would be wiped clean in the next downpour that would likely come by late afternoon.

As he jostled down the road, the long frond of a banana plant slapped his arm through the cab's open window. He knew to stay alert. Sometimes the plants reaching into the road could damage the truck or tear up his arm or face.

The meeting with Minister Tombu and Adrian Guerra had gone no better than Jim expected. The World Bank and Minister Tombu disagreed on the need for family planning. Islamic imams and the Catholic Church both opposed family planning that included birth control and abortion. The government had to reckon with their influence and a citizenry that could not comprehend a need to manage population. With poverty, malaria and the AIDS epidemic holding the average life expectancy in the 40s and with one of every four children dying before the age of five, many Leoneans strongly opposed programs that encouraged both abortion and other, more pro-active, means of birth control. In spite of that, the World Bank wanted to impose a UN-monitored family planning program in exchange for funding the malaria project No matter what decision Tombu made, he risked making a lot of people unhappy.

"It's not about babies," Tombu had said in the meeting. "It's about African investment. European master planners think we need to scale down our populations to increase productivity. Today, there are far too many Africans, and far too many sick ones. It costs the continent tens of billions in productivity and health care. Even the Africans want to reduce the numbers."

The three men had been sitting in Tombu's office at the State House.

"Which Africans?" Jim asked.

"Those who believe productivity and return on investment best measure a nation and its people. The ones who have lost touch with our history and traditions. They willingly throw that all away to make money and build fine homes for themselves. Sometimes, they're warlords like those we fight here. Sometimes, they lead countries, like Charles Taylor did in Liberia."

Adrian Guerra argued the World Bank side. "Population can't go unchecked," he said. "Sierra Leone needs to recover from the war. Resources are extremely limited."

"We know what the Catholics think," Tombu responded, nodding toward Jim. "But the politics are bigger than that. The imams are in the same camp. They quote the Koran 'You are my people, multiply.' They believe it is the duty of God to take care of the family. It's insulting for Europeans to bring family planning and say, 'You have a large population, you will have consequences.'"

"The population should be at the heart of all development, Minister," Guerra replied. "Five children per Leonean woman? No country in the world has developed themselves with a birth rate that high. Failing to implement a population-management plan would simply be irresponsible."

Tombu's forehead muscles tightened over the bridge of his nose, cold eyes peering out from under thick eyebrows. "And the World Bank does not give grants or loans to irresponsible regimes?" Tombu said.

"Minister, you act as though that's not the only choice."

"Adrian, you equate irresponsibility with moral backbone. My government believes in the sanctity of life as a fundamental principle. Pragmatically, a population of five million does not threaten the wealth of the world, nor could it conceivably use enough resources to disable future generations. Not with all the unoccupied land we have."

"What about the women? Would you deprive a woman of the choice of aborting a baby, allow her to die at child birth?"

Tombu leaned back in his chair. Two large French doors behind his desk opened onto a whitewashed veranda, five stories above a long expanse of green lawn and gardens that led from the State House toward the blue sea in the distance. Jim listened while Guerra pitched his case.

"Since when does every woman who does not abort her baby die at childbirth?" Tombu asked.

"Not all, but one in every twenty-three. How can you accept that?"

"I don't accept it. You need to help us fix the health care infrastructure needed to save those women. That's much bigger than family planning. We won't be able to backtrack, however, once we accept a culture of abortion."

"Think about it," Adrian responded. "One in twenty-three. The US is only one in 2400. It's more than one hundred times worse here. Not stopping it amounts to genocide."

"So you would have us kill the children to save the mothers."

"Yes. Sometimes."

"Let's apply that logic. Over 200 boys, ex-child soldiers, live in halfway houses down the road. Though forced into service, they still learned to kill recklessly. Many people have expressed concern that some will kill again. They say that once killing is in your system, you can never get it out. If a citizen feels threatened by the possibility an ex-child soldier might kill him or her, do they have the right to kill the child soldiers to offset that risk? Should the government just execute all of them?"

Guerra shifted in his chair, crossing his legs and wrapping his hands around a knee. "Totally different issue, Minister. A woman is dealing with her own body. A citizen is not in control of the people around him."

"So a woman controls her own body?"

"Yes, she does."

"For how long? 45 years? That's the life expectancy of a Leonean woman today."

"Then for 45 years."

"Adrian, control is an illusion. We don't control much of anything. And since when is her body and her baby's body not part of the communal body of our nation? Since when is the individual more important than the community? The individual is about today only. The community is about both today and the future. The rebel leader Foday thought he was more important than the community of our nation. It brought riches to him and a decade of civil war to everyone. And he died in prison, a broken man."

Guerra reddened, clearly not liking the comparison to the mass killer Foday. "You're comparing apples and oranges. Bottom-line is that you want the World Bank to risk assets on piloting a malaria vaccine here – one that you know will save hundreds of thousands here alone over the next five years. If you expect us to take that risk, then you need to show us that yours is a responsible regime."

Tombu rolled his chair closer to the long teak tabletop that acted as his desk. He folded his hands on the edge of the thick polished wood. "Then just help us deploy insecticide-treated nets for every child under five. That will be a lot less expensive for you and we won't have to sacrifice our souls to your bankers."

Tombu and Guerra glared at each other. Guerra leaned back in his chair. "Fine, Minister. That should reduce the death toll by... I believe the World Health Organization's number is 17%. What about the other 83% that you could save by playing ball? Would they make the same decision as you?"

"Adrian, if you withhold the vaccine, you're making the decision. Not me."

"Think it through," Adrian countered. "Sierra Leone will never get to the level of productivity needed for a thriving economy if it stays this sick. And you and I both know there's evidence that malaria and AIDS feed on each other. You're not only talking about economic impact, you're talking about a catastrophe that will make the civil war look like a picnic. The malaria-HIV combo is your black plague."

"I won't let that happen."

"Then work with me."

"You're asking me to play God," Tombu said.

Guerra leaned forward and looked hard into the minister's dark eyes. "That's right. And you may be the only real God these people have, Minister.

Look around your country. Where is God in all this?"

Jim interjected. "You're confusing God with Santa Claus, Adrian."

Guerra answered Jim with his eyes still on Tombu. "Father, why are you even here? This is about the health and finances of a nation, not some soft churchy thing."

"That's exactly why I'm here."

Guerra turned to face him. "You don't understand. In the greater scheme of things, you and what you do are disposable. A diversion for the masses. Don't cross me on this."

Jim's eyes widened briefly in surprise before he resumed his unflappable demeanor. "I've been threatened by much scarier people than you, Adrian."

"Maybe you'll think about it differently when you realize you're putting your friends in jeopardy, too."

"And how is that?"

Guerra tightened his lips and glanced toward the health minister who watched with interest. "You're not worth the time right now," he said to the priest.

"I'll pray for ya," the priest said his brogue coming out.

"Superstition won't help anyone."

Tombu stood and leaned across his desk toward his guests. "Gentlemen, let's not try to resolve the mysteries of faith right now. I have a busy day ahead."

"It's not about religion and mysteries," Guerra said. "It's about lives and numbers. You have no choice but to consider family planning?"

"It will take further time and thought," he answered.

"Don't let Fr Jim's church and the Islamic imams lead you down the wrong path."

"They speak for the unborn," Tombu said. "The unborn are the future. I have to listen."

"And I speak for the women dying today and for the 80,000 Leoneans who will die of malaria in the next twelve months without the vaccine."

Tombu nodded his acknowledgment.

Guerra stood to leave. "We need a decision within the week."

After Guerra left, Jim remained behind. "He's not havin' a good day," he said.

"Seemed like he was threatening you, Father. I'd take it seriously. These world order types actually have real power and wield it in some nasty ways. The part about your friends troubled me."

"I don't think his bosses at the World Bank would approve of his behavior. There's somethin' else goin' on with that one."

"Maybe. Bears watching."

"So what will you do?" Jim asked.

"About family planning? Not sure I have much choice. I'm the minister of health. I play God with people's well-being. I can condemn them or grant them life."

"The babies?"

"The living. The bird-in-hand. I'm given a choice between 80,000 certain malaria deaths a year or a potential wave of abortion deaths that will never stop. Neither one is a winning hand."

"Never thought of you as a glass half empty kind of guy." Jim attempted a smile. He looked out the doorway toward the sea. "Looks like we're in for some weather." He stepped on to the veranda. Clouds billowed into thunderheads over Cockerill Bay and the eastern Atlantic Ocean, the sea beneath them turning gray-green and filling with white caps. He moved his eyes closer to shore, resting them on the clear aquamarine waters and glistening white sand of the beach, still soaked in mid-day sunlight.

He spoke as he pondered the shoreline. "I'm a priest, William. I believe in the sanctity of life. I believe abortion is wrong." He drummed his fingers on the rail and lifted his eyes to the darkening horizon. "Yet letting one in twenty-three woman die in childbirth is not exactly in the spirit of preserving the sanctity of life. If we had infinite funds and time, we could flood the streets and the villages with doctors, nurses and modern equipment. We don't have infinite funds and time. Right now, women all around us are dying painfully as they bring life into the world."

Tombu remained in his chair, revolving it to look on Jim's back as he leaned on the veranda rail. Lightning flashed over the bay, a rumble of thunder following seconds later. "I know there's a good possibility we can save 80,000 per year with the malaria vaccine," he said. "Maybe we have to trust ourselves that we will not be like westerners and allow abortion to be abused as a means of birth control. We need to find the means to build the infrastructure to save these mothers in other ways and allow them to raise their children."

Jim turned back toward Tombu. "Adrian's telling us the World Bank will help provide that infrastructure if you allow family planning."

"The math's compelling. One in five children die by age five. The same medical infrastructure that will reduce maternal deaths should also reduce that number. And many of those children die from malaria. We can change that."

Jim stood silhouetted in the doorway as thunder rumbled and the sky flashed behind him. He said nothing.

"What does your conscience say, Father?"

"Jesus was about love," Jim responded, his words carefully paced as he thought them through. "I don't think he would refer to a rule book or pronouncements made thousands of miles away. He would somehow embrace every woman and every baby individually with love."

The men studied one another for half a minute. Tombu finally stood and walked to the veranda, sunlight replaced now with a dreary slate blue pall. Jim joined him. The two men stood together at the rail, eyes out to sea following seagulls buffeted violently by the wind as they glided above storm-tossed waves. A sudden blast of cooler air whipped onto the veranda as the storm's powerful gust line reached the State House.

"I don't know how to be Jesus, Father," the minister said, the first drops of rain splashing on to his face. "Do you?"

An explosion in the road ahead jerked Jim back to the present.

CHAPTER 18

Freetown Peninsula, Lokoma Road
October 18, 3:05 pm GMT

Jim swerved the pick-up to avoid the flying shrapnel. Bent green banana leaves and ferns slapped against the windshield. Shifting into reverse, he tried to back around to head in the other direction. Instead, another explosion went off behind him. He had driven into the middle of a firefight.

Only when armed teenagers in torn t-shirts, shorts, and flip-flops surrounded his truck did he realize the explosions targeted him. They waved Kalashnikov AK-47s around like boys elsewhere wave plastic swords or whiffle ball bats on the playground. They had no concept of the fragility and value of individual lives, not even their own.

Slowly, one hand in the air, Jim reached into his glove compartment and pulled out the roman collar that identified him as a priest. Often the rebel bands, particularly the ones from the countryside, would not cause trouble for a man of God for fear of spiritual retribution.

Stepping out of the truck, he reached through the collar of his shirt and pulled out a wooden cross that hung around his neck on a loop of string. He showed it and the collar to the boys.

The boys looked at each other and nodded all around. One of them stepped toward Jim.

"You're a priest? Fr. Reilly?"

Jim relaxed. They needed his help. These boys had come specifically for him. "Yes," he answered.

The group closed in.

"You work with the Lokoma?"

They tightened the circle around him. They were preparing to attack. Fear cut through him. The boy pressed the muzzle of his weapon under Jim's chin, tilting his head back and forcing him to rise on his toes. The boy's nostrils widened, his lips curled.

"Answer, priest."

"I do," he said, lifting his thoughts heavenward, remembering Christ's tortured death and how his own would be much quicker. Then, he thought about the baggie of quinine sulphate tablets he had in his pocket for Sara. "I'll make this easy if you do one small thing for me," he said, shoving the muzzle of the gun to the side and straightening to his full height, at least four inches taller than the tallest boy. "A little girl's life is at stake."

He stuck a hand in his shirt pocket to pull out the pill packet. The boy in front of him pulled the weapon back and raised it over his shoulder. He swung down hard at the side of Jim's head. The priest ducked, blocking the stock with his left forearm. The other boys advanced, striking wherever they could with their Kalashnikovs. Jim weaved, his arms flying in a desperate flurry to protect his head, but the numbers worked against him. The body blows quickly took their toll. He crumpled to the ground in stages, finally lying dazed on his stomach. He stared at the calloused feet of one of the boys, expecting a kick to the face, struggling to summon the strength to pull his arms over his head. Before he could move the surprising weight of his limbs, another blow, this time to the base of his skull, plunged him into darkness.

A piece of white dress, one edge aflame, lay on the cobblestones, only steps from him. Gasping, his ears popped.
"...bloody idiot!" a boy shouted.
The anguished wails of a man pierced the nightmare.

CHAPTER 19

Cameron Pass, Aldrich Mountain Lab
October 19, 1 pm Mountain Time

Sheila could not believe that Evan Conger knew who she was. She had been a rookie when he left five years earlier. Now, as she had hoped when she heard of his planned visit, he stood at her cubicle, towering over her at 6'4". She never understood how a younger woman could fall for a much older man, but Conger looked elegant, sexy. Powerful.

She always told herself she would never fall for money or power, but this silver-haired man with the chiseled face, kind blue eyes and the deep, calming voice – she wanted to curl up against his suit coat. Daddy fixation, she scolded herself. She knew her own father as ultimately a powerless man chewed up in corporate demands before a stroke put him in a nursing home for life. A fifty-something white-haired man in a wheel chair, struggling to get out from behind wide and frustrated eyes, Ernie Stratemeier could not write or speak, but clearly understood everything said to him.

She blinked away the vision of her dad and re-focused on her visitor.

"Claire tells me you're doing excellent work," he said.

"Claire is very kind. A lot of us push very hard. We're determined to see HIV and malaria eradicated."

"Within reach?"

Sheila glanced at Claire and Eldridge who stood on either side of Conger, Eldridge a few inches shorter, Claire almost diminutive at 5'5". Both looked steadily at her, waiting for the appropriate answer.

"We're very compartmentalized in function, so only Eldridge or Claire can offer complete perspective."

"Dr. Conger has an NDA agreement with us," McQuaid said. "You can speak freely."

A non-disclosure agreement. To Sheila, that meant she could peel another layer from the onion, but she knew that McQuaid and Eldridge both expected her to limit even that.

"I'm focused 100% on the HIV cure."

"Are you in trials?"

Eldridge jumped in. "We are. Tests here in the US have not been promising, but we hypothesize a mutational path that will open the door to complete eradication."

"I don't understand."

Eldridge grabbed a yellow pad from Sheila's desk and flipped to a blank page. He drew on the page, lining up several circles on top of one another and labeled them "HIV B," "HIV C," "HIVn." He drew an arrow from HIV B to another circle that he labeled "HIV B_1."

"A large body of research has uncovered a consistent path of migration among HIV mutations or clades. It follows that the older the origin of the HIV in the local human population, the further along the mutation. It is also predictable that the clades will become more virulent as they mutate, breaking down the body's defenses faster. This results in much shorter incubation periods and more rapid morbidity. Assuming HIV B is the oldest clade, it becomes HIV B_1. "

Eldridge drew a chart, showing successively decreasing survival periods for the mutations HIV B_1, HIV B_2, and HIV B_{N+1}.

Sheila watched as Conger contemplated the sketch. She knew he would notice that the line representing the time from infection to death grew shorter for each new mutation. That was an important underlying theme in the Aldrich strategy.

"My God," he said. "It's going to get much worse."

Eldridge nodded. "Much, much worse."

"What you're describing is provable based on what happened with smallpox, polio, and certain strains of flu," Conger said. "Even malaria. But the theory does not compensate for improved human immune adaptation and pharmacological intervention."

Claire interrupted. "Evan, almost by definition, HIV transcends human adaptation because of its long incubation cycle. That's the genius of it. Like a Trojan horse, it actually becomes the human immune adaptation, fooling the body's defenses into neutralizing themselves, accepting HIV cells as a part of the body's own defense system, a part not to be rejected. The body's disease-fighting T-cells think the HIV cell is just another T-cell and they let it alone. It's because the HIV attack moves at such a slow place. A little like the old saw about putting a frog in boiling water. If you throw the frog in boiling water, it jumps out. If you put it in cool water and gradually raise the temperature to boiling, the frog gets cooked."

Conger turned back to Sheila. "So where does this fit in with your research?"

"What we've designed is a form of pharmaceutical judo," Sheila explained. "We roll with the direction the disease is heading. We accept the deadly course of mutation and meet it when it gets there. That's the only way to beat this thing.

"We actually want the virus to mutate to where it breaks down T-cell walls so fast that the surviving T-cells have no time to adapt and accept HIV. They recognize the fast-moving mutation as disease. That makes the virus kill more quickly, but also much more vulnerable because the surviving T-cells will still attempt to reject HIV rather than accommodate it.

"There's still a big problem though because the T-cells, though alerted, don't know how to fight this disease. They need a weapon to conquer HIV at this stage so that the body develops permanent antibodies that defeat any future attack of the virus. And HIV loses its adaptability, the very thing that keeps science from defeating it."

Conger slowly rubbed his chin with his right hand. "So if we were sure that the body could adapt to defeat the downstream mutation, we'd want to encourage rapid mutation," he said.

Sheila felt a bubble of pride in her throat as Conger focused his attention on what she had to say. "Arguably. But with HIV we have no confidence that the body will adapt sufficiently on its own. My life for the last several years has been dedicated to developing a drug that will ensure that it does. Then, we can take the antibodies from those first successful cases and create vaccines with them."

"Why wouldn't you synthesize the antibodies?"

"Ultimately, we would," Claire said. "But there's no better drug factory than the human body if we can harness it."

"What's the catch?" Conger asked.

"Finding the mutation," Eldridge answered. "Sheila and her team have this thing far enough along that they would have a viable vaccine in place within 90 days of getting the first samples."

"How far away do you think that is?"

Sheila curled her lower lip under her teeth, restraining herself. Conger gave her a puzzled look. From over Conger's shoulder, Claire glared at her protégé.

"Soon," Claire answered. "Very soon. We expect it to arise somewhere in Central or West Africa. That's the general area where it is thought that humans consumed monkeys that carried the simian virus that became HIV. If we track the mutations from that theoretical point of origin, the progression indicates it could be only a matter of a few years, maybe even months, before someone is discovered with an adequately virulent mutation to test our theory. It is, in fact, very possible that there are people dying because of this new form now, but it just hasn't been identified. You know better than any of us how inadequate diagnostics are in that region."

Conger folded his hands. He looked back at Sheila. His gaze paused on her. She hoped he noticed her discomfort, but he quickly turned his attention back to the group. "Interestingly, the civil wars have prevented the kind of data collection and research that would find this mutation," Conger commented. "And because people die so fast, you wouldn't have the telltale lingering malaise normally found in HIV. Have you looked for spikes in morbidity from opportunistic diseases? It would make sense that those would be good areas to look."

Claire nodded her head affirmatively as she spoke. "We did a great deal of demographic research on that over the last several years, but the extent of the killing in the region masks any potentially revealing data. If there were to be a spike in young-adult malaria deaths, for example, it would be hard to pin down because so many of the potential victims are likely to have died first from violence. And even if there were a way to cut through that layer, many people in the region no longer have access to professional medical care, preventing both diagnosis and tracking."

"What about hospital records?" Conger asked.

"Nothing within hundreds of miles of Sierra Leone," Eldridge said. "The wars have shut everything down, and records were either lost or destroyed in the few hospitals left standing. We're starting with a clean slate for data. It will take years to get enough of it to do an appropriate spike analysis."

"So how do we get resources in the bush to sample enough of the population to find this mutation – if it exists?"

"The PDNA from Prodeus," McQuaid said. "They're deploying their portable DNA analyzers with the malaria vaccine pilot in Sierra Leone. Aldrich firmware is in them. Not only do we analyze the individuals DNA, but we can analyze the DNA of their T-cells and detect any early mutation factors. If we don't find the mutation, we'll know where they're going to show up."

"Wow," Conger whispered. "Does Dave Clement understand all this?"

"No, he has no need to know. He thinks he and Prodeus are providing a means to prove we're not planting HIV or some magic infertility pill in the malaria vaccine. This theory is both too revolutionary and potentially too profitable to disclose it outside a very small circle of necessary people."

"I've known him a long time and we just spent a day together in the bush of Sierra Leone. He's a bright man. Don't underestimate him. My guess is he'll figure out your game plan sooner rather than later."

He turned to Sheila. "You have millions of lives in your hands, Sheila. This is remarkable work."

"Thank you, Doctor." Sheila reached out her right hand to shake Conger's. She held his hand tightly, staring hard into his eyes. She pushed a small flash drive into his palm. He looked at her curiously. She pressed her lips together long enough to communicate a message of confidentiality. The doctor withdrew his hand and placed it in his coat pocket.

"Please come by any time," Sheila said.

"I'm sure we'll have an opportunity to talk again," Conger said. He patted his coat pocket, giving Sheila a slight nod.

Claire and Eldridge guided him away from Sheila's cubicle on to the next phase of the tour.

Claire looked back and gave Sheila a thumbs-up sign. As soon as they turned the corner, Sheila dropped into her chair, relief exploding from her lips.

CHAPTER 20

Poudre River Canyon - 27 miles west of Fort Collins
October 20, 11:30 am Mountain Time

Jennifer rolled her windows down and sucked in a deep breath of cold morning air. Another day of powering through at the office lay ahead of her. Glancing at herself in the rearview, she saw a pale face that had spent way too much time indoors. In the ten years since she had gone to work full time in the cubicle filled world of nerds and Dilberts, she had come to take her sex appeal for granted. Her continued failure to entice Dave now had her second guessing herself like a high school freshman. Her face needed some color.

For distraction, she turned the radio on as she waited at a red light. The weather forecast caught her attention. The Fort Collins high temperature would break 80 degrees, eight shy of the all-time October record, but still unseasonably warm. As the light changed to green, another light went on in her head. She pressed her speed dial for Sheila.

Two hours later, she and Sheila sunned themselves in the canyon alongside the white-water rapids of the Poudre River, midway between Sheila's lab in Cameron Pass and Jennifer's office in Loveland. Just a few days earlier, it had snowed four inches in Fort Collins. Now the thermometer registered 76 degrees after a low of only 42 the night before. Jennifer reveled in this weather. She looked skyward where the northern Colorado Rockies displayed only a thin coat of snow and the silver-white ribbons of retreating glaciers against a massive backdrop of dry purple and gray rock faces. Wisps of white clouds entwined peaks silhouetted against a deep blue sky. Except for the snow earlier in the week – now melted at any altitude below 8,500 feet – drought conditions prevailed into their fourth month. On the Front Range, 25 miles distant from where they lounged and over 1,000 feet lower, the grass had been pre-maturely brown for months, scorched black in spots by brush fires.

Jennifer closed her eyes and listened to the Poudre River descending over rapids less than ten yards from where she and Sheila lounged. The Poudre originated at the Continental Divide, nearly 4,000 feet higher up, just west of the Trail Ridge Visitors Center in Rocky Mountain National Park. From those origins, its icy waters flowed into the Missouri River and then the Mississippi to help make that river the longest and widest in North America.

But today it provided secluded shoreline for the two beach-hungry women, both too long buried in the day-to-day routines and stresses of their jobs. Their personal droughts from relaxation had both lasted longer than the Rockies' rainfall drought.

Stretched out on cheap folding beach chairs that Jennifer purchased at the K-Mart in Fort Collins on the way up that morning, they relaxed with light beer, digesting small burgers prepared on a portable grill. Behind the cover of enormous boulders, their pale bodies, naked except for bikini bottoms, absorbed intense mountain sun. A very light breeze dried small beads of sweat on their warm skin almost as soon as they formed. The smell of coconut and pineapple from suntan lotion, with too low an SPF, transported them emotionally to the ocean.

Jennifer handed her friend another Sunshine Wheat beer from Fort Collins' own New Belgium Brewery. Sheila pulled the tab; honey-toned ale splattered all over her face and chest, a foamy rivulet flowing between the small mounds of her meager bosom before finally settling in the well of her navel.

"Suntan lotion," she laughed as she tried to cup the spilled beer in her hands and drink it.

The two women met seven years earlier at the Boulder Lab of the Aldrich as young recruits fresh from grad school. Change quickly overtook the place soon after they started.

Within weeks of their arrival, Evan Conger, the lab's executive director, left the Aldrich to join Will Bentley's Presidential administration as Surgeon General. Claire McQuaid replaced him, and the two women hoped that the recruitment of a woman director would bode well for them. Instead, McQuaid, overcompensating so as not to appear to favor women, kept Sheila and Jennifer under non-stop pressure. The two rookies recovered from long days by spending a lot of late evenings taste-testing the products of Northern Colorado's microbreweries, sharing confidences and building trust.

In the daytime, Sheila broke down the genome, focusing specifically on third-world genetic pre-dispositions to infectious diseases such as malaria, dengue fever, and HIV. Jennifer, both a gifted research scientist and biostatistician, built elaborate statistical models of where certain conditions prevailed, doing concentration studies to ascertain where given conditions dominated. In her third year at the Aldrich, directed by Claire, she began the earliest in-depth work on the progression of HIV, starting with the Simian Immuno Virus (SIV), hypothesizing that man had been infected by simians, or apes, as early as the 1930s.

Then things grew even more intense. Claire recruited Eldridge Perry to run drug discovery in the heavily secured mountain lab in Cameron Pass. Both Jennifer and Sheila transferred to Perry's team where they found their work compartmentalized on the paranoid research campus. Neither was clear as to how the activities of others in the lab connected with their own activities. Teams were proscribed from discussing their work with other teams.

Her progression-analysis work soon allowed Jennifer to branch off to develop tracking software for fieldwork. She contracted with Ed Hepp, a consultant in Loveland, 30 miles north of Boulder, to create genome-analysis software to meet the project's requirements. This led to Hepp meeting Claire McQuaid and the development of a strategic alliance. Hepp, Claire, Jennifer, and a small team of bio-engineers soon conceived a portable analysis unit for field deployment, its magic embedded in firmware written jointly by Aldrich and Prodeus engineers, leveraging the separate skill sets. The portable DNA analyzer was born. Suddenly Hepp had a very interesting business with Claire as shareholder, board member, and advocate with the investment banking community.

Jennifer helped Hepp recruit Dave Clement, the best business development exec in the business according to Evan Conger, and then joined Prodeus herself with a promise of stock options amounting to 1% of the company. Since leaving for Prodeus, Jennifer stayed in touch with Sheila socially, but discussed very little work.

Sheila finished licking the beer off her fingertips and took a long swig from the can.

"You're so delicate, Dr. Stratemeier," Jennifer teased as she rolled onto her stomach to tan her back.

"It's the Pittsburgh in me. Your Texas class never did rub off on me."

They giggled. Then, they lay quietly listening to the ruffling of golden aspen leaves in the breeze and the gentle pulsations of water rushing over and between rocks.

After a few minutes, Sheila rolled over, adjusting her bikini bottom for maximum exposure. She knew she would not expose this skin to sun again for months.

"Jenn," Sheila said quietly, unsure if her friend was awake.

"Hmmm?" Jennifer replied, mellow from a slight beer buzz and the natural sedative of basking in the sun.

"Evan Conger visited the lab yesterday."

"How was that?"

"I forgot what an elegant man he is."

"You're not falling for an old guy like that."

"No. Plus he's married. Happily."

"You should be able to fix that."

Sheila wiped off a rivulet of sweat that tickled her side. "Your style," she responded. "Not mine."

"It's the 21st century, bitch. It's cool to be a 'ho.'"

"The lab is the only significant other I have time for."

"I get it," Jennifer replied. "I'd love to see him again, though. His mind is so amazing. I always thought I'd get to work closely with him at the Aldrich. Then he ended up surgeon general."

"McQuaid's not a bad replacement."

"Perry is."

"He's a management layer is all. I can deal with him."

"I deal with him on the Prodeus side of the joint venture, but I prefer to deal with Claire whenever possible. The man's weird."

They sat silently for a few minutes, the rush of water and the calls of birds forming a peaceful backdrop.

"Do you think Conger can be trusted?" Sheila asked.

"In what way?"

"Ethics. Confidences."

Jennifer lifted her head to look at Sheila. "Where are you going with this?"

A hawk circled overhead. Sheila watched it glide effortlessly between the cliffs. "Ever get paranoid?" she asked, still watching the hawk.

"Sure. What's that have to do with Conger?"

Sheila closed her eyes and shifted on the beach chair. "I don't think it does," she mumbled. "I lost my train of thought."

Jennifer waited for further comment, but none came for several minutes. Finally, Sheila spoke again. "Trusting Conger's not a bad move, right?"

Jennifer pressed her elbows on the straps of the beach chair and pushed herself up into a sitting position. "You must have told him something you shouldn't have."

Sheila lay on her stomach, facing away from Jennifer. She said nothing.

"What are you afraid of?"

Sheila hesitated. "There's something going on at the lab," she said after a long beat. "Some kind of Nazi thing. We're on task in a literal sense, but the interpretation of mission is out of whack. The spirit of this thing doesn't match up to what you and I think we're doing."

"What's to interpret?" Jennifer said. "It's pretty straightforward."

Sheila rolled over and sat up on the edge of the flimsy beach chair, her legs splayed indelicately. The inner thigh high up on her right leg immediately drew Jennifer's eye.

"What's that?" Jennifer asked, nodding toward what looked like a brand about half an inch high by one inch long just beneath the crease where her inner thigh met her torso.

Sheila defensively cupped a hand over the spot.

"Is that a tattoo?" Jennifer said, rising to her feet.

"No," Sheila said, pinching her legs together. "It's just a… a bruise."

But Jennifer was on her, trying to spread her friend's knees. "What does it say? It was letters. I saw that. Oh my God, Sheila! You have a man's name tattooed between your legs!"

Sheila kicked at Jennifer and rolled onto the ground. As she did, Jennifer got one arm underneath her leg, and Sheila found herself spread-eagled face down on the ground. Jennifer now had a good view of the tattoo.

"Rocky 28714," read the ink etched on the soft, pink skin near the top of her thigh. Jumping to her feet, Jennifer stood over Sheila. "Is that a phone number? A man's phone number?"

Sheila rolled onto her back, looking at the clear blue sky overhead. "An indiscretion."

"A recent one?"

"No, I've had it for a while."

"Sheila, we've shared locker rooms. We've had saunas together. I would have seen this."

"I didn't know you cared." Sheila tried to change the subject.

"I'm serious."

Heaving a deep breath, Sheila covered her eyes with her hands. "I got drunk. The guy broke my heart. I didn't want to forget him, but I wanted to reduce him to a number. My own little way of demeaning him."

"How come I never heard about this guy?"

"I fell fast. And he broke up with me just as fast. Once I got the tattoo, I didn't want to think about him again. I guess I figured I could start a movement of women who memorized the scum's number as a secret code to join the anti-scum club."

"You were more than just very drunk."

"Extremely. Completely pissed. Semantics."

"I'm not buying it. There's more going on here."

"Maybe, but that's all you get. Rocky 28714"

"If you can't trust me, then who?"

"I don't trust anyone." Sheila fixed a stare on Jennifer that said she was clearly done with the subject. Awkward silence followed until Jennifer brought the conversation back to where it was before the tattoo came up.

"So what's this about something bad?" she asked. "Did you tell Conger about it?"

Sheila rolled onto her side, grabbed another beer, popped the top more cautiously than last time, and sipped.

"No. I'm just paranoid."

"Sheila, you need to tell me what's going on with you."

Sheila sipped the beer again. "Maybe Conger could help me figure it out. That's all I was thinking."

"You told him something."

"No. I'm just not connecting my thoughts this afternoon. It's the beer." She looked down at her body. Dirt from the brief wrestling match on the ground, mixed with her sweat and tanning lotion, had turned to mud on her skin. Running her fingers down her abdomen to see if the gunk would come off, she left a slimy, sweeping handprint that ran from her rib cage to the top of her bikini bottom.

"That looks obscene," Jennifer remarked.

"Yecch," Sheila said. "Be right back."

Putting down the can, she stood and splashed into the shallow rapids on the edge of the river. As she high-stepped into the 52-degree water, goose bumps radiated in all directions. She squealed as she danced around in the frigid stream.

"Get in here!" she called over the noise of the rapids.

Jennifer tried unsuccessfully to rub the mud off her own legs, forearms, and belly. Giving up, she grabbed a towel and sat on a rock at the edge of the river.

"It's refreshing," called Sheila as she tried to splash her friend from ten feet away.

"You're out of your mind," Jennifer replied. "Your goose bumps are bigger than your boobs. C'mon out. You can dry off with this."

Glowing pink, Sheila sloshed out of the water and leaned against the side of the rock on which Jennifer sat. An instant later, she pushed her squealing friend into the water. Slipping on stones and stumbling through mud, Jennifer exited the river spluttering but clean. Invigorated by the cold, she laughed uncontrollably with the only close friend she had since college.

Jennifer made no further attempts to pry out information. And Sheila did not bring it up again.

Clouds rolled in half an hour later bringing a chill. The women parted.

On the drive back up the Poudre Canyon to the lab, Sheila wondered if she had said too much. Or not enough. Jennifer had seen the tattoo. Sheila felt confident that Jennifer knew her well enough to know it was more significant than she let on.

She pulled on to the road's narrow shoulder and stopped. She thought about chasing Jennifer down to… Explain? Make sure she would help her and not betray her? She had intended to give Jennifer some breadcrumbs, but found herself wanting to confide everything. Instead, she had stuck with her plan and leaked only tidbits, concerned about putting her friend in the middle, concerned that she might offer information that could force Jennifer to betray their friendship.

She looked at her watch. They had parted 20 minutes earlier. Jennifer would be more than halfway to where Route 14 fed into 287 in the geological bowl that rolled into Fort Collins at the eastern edge of the Rockies. Sheila would never be able to catch up. And she needed to get back to the lab.

As she pressed the gas pedal and drove back on to the road, Sheila wondered if she had been too subtle about the tattoo. She wanted it to be a memorable moment for her friend. An insurance policy. But part of her still worried that giving Jennifer any information was a mistake.

And a very dangerous one.

CHAPTER 21

Loveland, Colorado, Prodeus Office
October 21, 9:52 am Mountain Time

Dave keyed in his credentials for the Amazon cloud service that he and Sheila used. He clicked on NewMeds, their only document folder. No one else knew about this communication backchannel. The Aldrich tracked all of Sheila's emails, texts and social media activities. On the other hand, the cloud, on servers owned and protected by one of the world's biggest and most security conscious companies, left no obvious trace on Sheila's phone or on Aldrich servers, although someone who plodded through the immense server logs item by item might ultimately find it. Dave did not want anyone to know about Liv's illness and Sheila did not want Claire McQuaid or Eldridge Perry to know that she took time away from her job to help out.

A text file dated today's date, October 21, appeared on the list. Finally, Dave thought. The last contact had been a simple acknowledgment of Dave's anxiety ten days earlier.

I have news for Liv, Dave. It's too delicate for online delivery so we should meet. I don't think even Claire's fascist security team will find our cloud files, but I'd rather play it extremely safe. I'll be down on the Front Range for meetings at Aldrich HQs in Boulder on the morning of the 28th. Can you meet for coffee first thing before I go into the office?. Bottom-line: I have what you're looking for, but it's complicated.

What he was looking for was an outright cure that would eradicate Liv's HIV. Sheila knew that. This must have meant that she found it.

Keeping his excitement in check, Dave looked up his calendar. The early morning of the 28th had a production meeting scheduled at 8. He would postpone it for this. He uploaded a note to Sheila suggesting 6:30 a.m. at the Eye Opener Coffee House in Niwot, a few miles north of Boulder. He would check the cloud again tonight to look for her confirmation.

Dave signed out of the service. Then he pumped his fist once in the air.

"Please, God," he said quietly.

Fort Collins; Clement Home
October 21, 10:15 am Mountain Time

The phone's trilling caused Mel to look at the caller ID. Dave. He had not been very good about spending time at home, but he sure called frequently from the office or the road, at least in the States. Usually, he talked about the business, about what was stressing him – instead of what was stressing her. Mel could do nothing but listen. When she offered advice, he made her feel stupid, pointing out that she did not understand some subtlety.

"You are intelligent, Mel," he would say. "I respect you. But it can only be expected that I'd understand my work better than you would."

Logic never helped. So she just listened, absorbing his stress, unable to do a damned thing about it. He knew this. Still, he called. He made her his stress repository. When he did stay in town, he inevitably made some comment close to bedtime about something stressful at the office.

"Hepp told me things weren't all smiles," he said on one occasion, muting the TV at the commercial break following Jimmy Fallon's monologue.

"When was this?"

"This morning. He called me in for it."

"He said exactly that?"

"Word for word."

"Could you end up losing this job, too?"

"I did the right thing, Mel. Genofot crossed the line."

"And you ran your mouth about it. You played Don Quixote and took on a well-funded corporation. What did that get us? Genofot's still in business. And you couldn't find a regular job for four years."

"And I used those four years to do consulting and build credibility with anyone who was anyone in the pharmaceutical world."

"That's right, Dave. But we never knew whether or not we'd make the next mortgage payment. One month, you'd have a consulting deal and the next month you had nothing. That's no way to live."

"I know. I promised you there would be no more tilting at windmills. I've kept that promise."

"I hope so. Sometimes I don't think you even know you're doing it." She glanced at the TV before turning her attention back to him. "So what's Ed's issue?"

"Cooperation with Claire McQuaid."

"Well, you don't like her. Maybe that's coming through."

"I like her enough. She just wants to control me. Wants to know everything is going to go exactly as she wants it when she wants it. That's not healthy in a joint-development activity. There has to be give and take. We're Claire's partner, not her employees. Hepp doesn't get it."

He persisted in calling him Hepp that night, not Ed. Mel always took that as a signal that Dave could be popping off at the office, filled with the self-righteousness of the combative college journalist he once was. Some kind of Messiah complex. The same complex that got him fired at Genofot.

"You need to roll with it, Dave," she said on that occasion. "Remember it's about the income, not proving Claire or Ed wrong."

"I can replace the income." He picked up the remote. "Fallon's doing late night hashtags," he said.

He turned off the mute. The sound of studio-audience laughter filled the bedroom. Mel sat up against her pillow, arms folded. He pressed a hand gently around her forearm.

"Sorry," he said. "I'll be smart about this. I promise. You don't have to give it another thought. I'm not going to lose this one. No Don Quixote act."

She fumed during the hashtag segment, both worried about Dave's job security and angry with him for bringing work up in bed. Laughing at Fallon, he nudged her when she failed to crack a smile. Pressed, she forced a small grin, but could tell he was pissed at her for not relaxing and enjoying the show. How could she possibly win?

Dave nodded off during the next commercial. The sound of applause for the next guest woke him. He reached up and turned off his bedside lamp. Rolling onto his side, he snuggled into his pillow and moved one of his feet over to touch her leg. She wanted to pull away, but his warmth felt comforting against her inevitably cold feet. Within a few minutes, he began snoring while Mel stewed, the din of the Tonight Show acting like white noise. Sometimes she did not get to sleep for hours on those nights; often, she spent part of those hours alternately wishing he would stop snoring or that he were still out of town.

After she threw him out of the house, she told him on the phone that she realized she could do nothing about any of the stress; she said that while he sometimes seemed to thrive on it, it was killing her. She absorbed stress about things over which she had no control at all, a very unhealthy situation.

The situation with Liv – compounded by Dave's work stress – left her in a continual state of anxiety, such that she had to constantly fight the compulsion to completely flip out. So she did things like exhaust herself on the bike trails in the pre-dawn hours, hoping to get her cortisol levels down and give herself a fighting chance against anxiety.

Dave's response to her stress: "Let it go."

What better way to piss her off.

Loveland, Colorado; Dave's Office
October 21, 10:15 a.m.

Dave pressed the phone to his ear. He had not called Mel since the morning he arrived back in Colorado. When he called that morning and in the preceding weeks, she did not answer or return his calls. He thought she probably dropped to her knees every day to thank God for caller ID.

But now he urgently wanted to speak with her. He wanted to tell her about Sheila's news, to tell her that he had mined for hope and found it. Sure, he had no details yet. But he had learned to breathe hope in fumes over the years, gasping for enough to drive the next step forward. Mel understood that and, with Liv's situation, absolutely understood it.

His fingers poised over her name on his phone. He wondered what the point was. She wouldn't answer and she wouldn't call back. Unless he left a specific message about Sheila's news. He would not do that. Since the Aldrich had a stake in Prodeus, he suspected their security team spied on him and his team as well.

Maybe she would pick up, though. Maybe if kept calling every five minutes, she would answer to at least tell him to stop. He stood and closed his office door. No sense in anyone overhearing his embarrassment when she did not answer, when he left his pleading message on the answering machine.

Sitting on the edge of the desk, he tapped her name and the phone dialed. Did he really even want her to pick up? Seemed like he never said the right thing anymore. He'd probably only make matters worse.

He asked himself how much worse it could get. She already must have turned Liv against him. Neither one of them would speak with him. Yet, he remained hopeful. What if she got angry with him for calling? What if his calls finally cut off all hope of reconciliation? If he lost that hope, he had nothing.

His index finger hovered over the red "end" button on the phone. He heard Mel's phone ringing on the other end. Three times. Four. Headed for voice mail one more time.

"Hi, Dave," she said.

His heart nearly thumped right through his chest wall. Her voice sounded different to him. New. Maybe it was the surprise of her picking up.

"Mel?"

"Who'd you expect? I don't have a secretary. It's me or voice mail."

"No. You. I wanted to talk with you."

He heard her fumbling with papers. He wanted to fill in the space; he feared he would say the wrong thing.

"How was your trip to West Africa?" she said after a moment.

"Okay. But I missed coming home to you and Liv."

"Liv missed you, too."

"What about you?"

"Not so much."

Dave had hoped for more. "I know I haven't made either of you enough of a priority. There are all sorts of business justifications, but in the end, I know I've been selfish."

She hesitated on the other end. He half expected her to launch into a tirade confirming his admission. She surprised him. "We've both had problems with our priorities," she said. "You were right. I'm part of the problem. I wanted the things you could buy with big success. Still do. It's just a lot clearer that there are certain things not worth giving up to get those things."

"Right about now, I think I understand that better than ever."

"I hope so, Dave."

"Me, too," he said quietly.

"So I lied. I do miss you."

"I want to move back home," he said.

"Baby steps, sweetie."

"We need to talk. It's important. About Liv."

"What is it?"

"Can't talk on the phone. Might be extra ears."

"Ok, James Bond. Any plans this evening?"

"No. None." He did not even check his calendar. He knew that he could let nothing take this chance away.

"Come to Liv's game. Go to dinner with us afterward."

"Sure. I'd love to. How's she doing?"

"Seems normal. The meds have things in check."

"Is she good about taking them?"

"I think so. I try to keep count, but it gets away from me. I need to put a chart inside the medicine cabinet and make a daily note."

"You have a lot on your plate, Mel. I should be there to help."

"Those West African witch doctors must have sent back a new Dave."

"I don't need a witch doctor to realize I could do things differently."

"I might need one to believe you."

"What time tonight?"

"Game's at 4:30 at the high school."

"I'll be there."

"On time?"

This time he glanced quickly at his calendar. "I have a 3:30 I shouldn't miss. A lot of people counting on me. Be okay if I'm a little late? "

He heard exasperation on the other end.

"How late?"

"Fifteen minutes?"

"You have thirty. No more."

"That's more than fair."

"See you then, Dave."

"I love you, Mel."

"Show me."

"I promise."

"I love you, too. Don't make me any sorrier than I already am for that."

"Not my plan," he said.

A click on the other end. He threw his fists into the air. God! That felt good! he thought.

He sat down, absent-mindedly pressing the arrow keys on his keyboard. Slowly his mind churned, turning his exultation into apprehension. After a moment, he leaned forward, elbows on the desk and held his head in his hands.

"Thank you, Lord," he mumbled. "Now, don't let me blow it."

CHAPTER 22

Dave's Office
October 21, 1:30 p.m. Mountain Time

Jennifer's tap on his door a few hours later brought bad news.

"Dammit," Dave said. He thrust his head back against the pad at the top of his oversized leather chair. "I can't believe I missed the conflict. Dammit!"

Only five minutes earlier, he listened to a voice mail from Mel reminding him about his commitment to be at the game. She reminded him that she and Liv loved him, that they were counting on him to take advantage of a chance at a fresh start.

Jennifer looked at him, concern on her face. "You have no options on this one, Dave. Geneva's a can't-miss event. Not that Liv's volleyball game isn't. But there are 300 people depending on you here. And their families. "

"For some reason, I thought I didn't leave until tomorrow night."

"Connecting flight's tomorrow. You probably just did a quick scan and saw that date. Conference is day after that."

He drummed his fingers on the desk. "I have a chance to move back home. There has to be a way to take a later flight to Geneva."

"I arranged for Evan Conger to meet you at the airport. He's counting on you now."

"When did that happen?"

"I thought you'd want that. He's putting you in front of the W-H-O committee responsible for the whole project. Plus he's just finished two days of meetings with the Aldrich. He'll have updates you want to hear."

"I do. I want his perspective. You're right."

"Tell Mel you'll have all the time in the world for them when you retire on the millions you're going to make for all of us. Two more years at most, according to you."

He smiled wanly. He knew he did not have two more days, let alone two more years, with Mel, not if he blew this one.

"If she loves you, she'll cut you a break on this. If she really loves you."

"She loves me," he said. "It's more complicated than that."

"Then how come she didn't take any of your calls until today. Why won't she let you see your daughter?"

Dave waved a hand in the air. He could think of a dozen reasons, but Jennifer did not warrant that much insight. Jennifer walked around the desk and sat on the edge close to his chair.

Same enticing scent. He noticed she wore a short skirt and no hose today. Her toned slender legs demonstrated the benefits of spending a lot of time doing cardio. She placed a gentle hand on his shoulder.

"You're a good man. She's making you forget that. That's a disservice to both of you. And to Liv. They need you to be confident to pull off the product launch and take this company public. We all do. We're counting on you to make the public offering successful."

"I don't question my business skills. But I don't want to make a sacrificial offering of my family in exchange for the public offering of this company's stock."

She now had a hand on each of his shoulders, her face within a foot of his. "Wake up, boss. I see you day in and day out. This thing has you distracted. It's blunting your edge."

"I have a shot to put my life back together."

"If she opened the door today, she'll open it again later. She's figured out that she needs you more than you need her."

"That's not true."

Jennifer adjusted her position on the desk, turning her bare knees toward Dave, a warm hand on his. "Dave, I'm a woman. I know women."

He freed his hand from her grasp. Standing, he walked to the window. He looked toward Longs Peak, but he did not see the mountains. He had worked so hard for so long. The brass ring stood just barely out of reach.

"I need to figure out how to cover both bases," he said, turning back around.

Jennifer nodded reassuringly and then picked her pad up from the desk. "Anne gave me the details of your travel itinerary before I walked in. Right now you're scheduled to lay over in Denver for 90 minutes. If you're willing to risk it, Anne can probably set you up with a 20-minute layover. You'll have to run from the commuter gate, but you can do it."

Just the thought of running through the terminal again winded Dave. It used to be easy. Travel, long hours – not to mention the normal processes of time – had all taken their toll. Still, nothing weighed in like his obsession with work. Exercise and healthy eating – as well as everything else – took a back seat. He marveled that Mel and Liv did not seem to understand what it took to run a business, especially an early stage deal with so much at stake. If they did, there would be no expectation for him to show up at girls' volleyball games or any other high school nonsense. Maybe not nonsense, but -

"Or you could just drive down," Jennifer suggested.

"That's a good idea," he said as his chest heaved. "Let's cancel the commuter. The drive's only an hour, maybe an hour and five. That would give me the time to see the entire game and have a quick dinner with them. I really need to do that."

"Puts a ton of pressure on you."

"The game starts at 4:30 and it's a 20 minute drive. I can do that. Flight out of Denver's at 8:40. So if I'm on the road by 6:30 worst case, I can park in short-term and make it."

"If the security line's not too bad."

"Won't be at that hour mid-week."

"I think you're pushing it," she said.

He shrugged. "I'm always pushing it."

"What about packing? Did you pack this morning?"

He walked to the door and called over a cubicle to his assistant. "Anne, upgrade to business class tonight, right?"

"Doesn't look promising. It's a Triple 7, though. Pretty roomy in coach."

"Not a bad option. Also, I need you to help get me out of my 3:30 meeting by 3:55 at the very latest."

"I'll try," his diminutive assistant said. Premised on his track record, he knew he had given her a daunting task. "And then there's a really big favor I need, too."

Anne rolled her chair out from under her desk and peeked around the partition.

"Can you to go to my apartment and pack some things for me?" He dangled his keys in front of her.

"Not a problem," she said as she took the keys.

"Oh, and Anne, can you make sure my boarding pass is delivered with my ticket. I won't have time to check in tonight."

Anne gave him the thumbs up and walked away. Jennifer walked up behind Dave at the door and brushed his backside with her hand. He turned to her, eyes wide.

"Sorry," she said. "Accident."

He tried to back out of the doorway, but Jennifer, facing him, squeezed by him before he could. She made full and inappropriate body contact in the tight space as she passed. "Later, Dave," she said as she headed into the sea of cubicles.

CHAPTER 23

Boulder, Colorado; Aldrich Institute Headquarters
October 21, 2:05 pm Mountain Time

The rage building in Claire's eyes caused Evan Conger to hesitate and assess.

"We represent the greatest hope Africa could imagine, Evan. How dare you sit in judgment of me!"

"I'm not judging you, Claire. I'm just concerned that you might be sacrificing people to save others."

"All depends on how you spin it, but it is, in fact, done all the time, Doctor high-and-mighty. That's a fundamental axiom of war."

"This is medicine. Healing. Not war, Claire."

"Wake up, Evan. This is absolutely war. More people die from malaria and HIV every year than are killed in wars and traffic accidents combined."

Evan rose from his chair opposite Claire's desk. He walked to her window and looked out at the Flatirons. When he occupied this office, gazing at them always brought him peace. The majesty of nature.

He turned back to her, only to find her right behind him.

"You need to look at the data," she said, handing him a note with a link, a sign-in name, and a password written on it.

"What will it tell me?"

Claire's green eyes, sparkling in the light from the window, displayed an inner calm now. "I know you think we're talking about killing people. You're wrong. We're saving people."

"That's not what I've been led to believe."

"Who told you that?"

He shook his head. "I can't tell you."

"Can't or won't?"

"I owe my sources confidentiality."

"Have you researched their information?"

"There hasn't been time. I've only had time to read a small portion of what I've been given."

Claire smiled. "So it must be someone here."

Evan could almost see her mind working, probably mentally listing everyone with whom he had contact during his visit of the last few days.

She walked back to her desk. "Do just one thing for me. We've both sat in the same chair. We both want the same thing for sub-Saharan Africa. So you owe me that much."

"What's that, Claire?"

"Sit in a spare office and sign in to that link. Look at the data and see if you get a better understanding of what we're really doing."

"I have a plane to catch."

"If you really think we're up to some kind of evil here, it would be worth missing the plane to talk us out of it. Wouldn't it?"

"I don't think you're up to any kind of evil, but I am concerned about your judgment from what I've seen on this trip."

She started walking out of the room. Evan did not move.

"Are you coming?" she said.

After depositing Evan in the spare office, Claire returned to her own office and locked the soundproof door. The list of possible leakers who knew enough to warn Evan Conger about the potential human toll made up a very small group. She collapsed in the chair behind her desk and made a call.

"Conger knows," she said into the phone. "There's a source inside our camp. We have to change the line-up. I need your confirmation."

She listened while the person on the other end recited details of the pre-arranged contingency, confirming that he understood the steps ahead.

"Good," she said. "Remember if anything about this points back in this direction, it's your ass." She hung up.

She choked back tears of frustration. So many years of careful hard work. No one could be allowed to interfere now. No one was indispensable. She started to call up her video, but felt dizzy and lay back in her chair instead.

"I won't let you down, Da," she said.

...She saw nothing, felt nothing. Her father's voice called out to them, but she couldn't answer. Then she felt the heat and the first inkling of a pain that came straight from hell itself.

CHAPTER 24

Fort Collins High School Gym
October 21, 3:15 p.m., Mountain Time

Mel leaned across the vehicle's console and kissed Liv good-bye. The girl let her mother's dry lips barely brush her cheek before pulling away. She pushed open the car door, dragging her gym bag off the floor. Glancing around, she reassured herself that no one had seen her mother's affection. No matter how many times Liv pulled this stunt, an almost daily ritual, Mel still felt a twinge of heartache. At least the girl remained affectionate at home – when she had no visitors.

Liv pushed the door shut but quickly cracked it open again.

"He's not going to let me down, is he?" she said, peering in.

"I told you what he said, Liv. I think he means it. He needs to mean it. He knows that now."

As Liv headed off into the locker room, Mel searched for a parking space. Be here, she thought. Just be here. She scanned the rows for Dave's Volvo, but it was too early. Best she could hope for would be for Dave to pull in right on time.

As she opened her door, she saw Janet Berwin, Chelsea's mom, walking by. "Hi, Janet."

Janet pretended not to hear. Unlike her tall and athletic daughter, Janet was a short, slender woman with cropped dark brown hair. Her complexion had died years earlier from too much smoking and membership in a tanning salon, although today Janet looked different. Her crow's feet and forehead wrinkles looked gone. Botox, thought Mel. A lot of it. But where did she get the money? And what was with the protruding duck lips?

"Janet!"

"Oh, hi, Mel."

Mel caught up with Janet and walked with her. Inverse to their daughters, the athletic Mel seemed to tower over Janet. The two women had been school-year pals since their girls started sleepovers together in the fourth grade. They had kept each other occupied at many birthday parties and school events, always tentatively supportive of each other.

"So how's the dating life?" Mel asked.

"What dating life?" Janet mumbled.

"You're just too picky."

"That's it. Three kids at home and a body bulging in the wrong places have nothing do with anything."

"Don't be so hard on yourself."

Janet shrugged. Mel felt an urge to tell her about Liv's situation, to help put things in perspective.

"So how come you're not driving the team to away games this year?" Janet asked. "I thought that was why you bought that SUV a few years back."

"Hasn't worked out this season."

"Chelsea told me Liv's been sick and missed a lot of games. Guess it doesn't make sense to drive when your kid's not going."

Mel slowed her pace. "No, I guess it doesn't."

"Is it the stress at home making her sick?" Janet asked.

"We're fine," Mel said.

"Really? I heard you joined the ranks of the single."

Mel stopped walking. She waited for Janet to stop and turn around. "Just taking a little break. Doesn't look like a long-term problem."

"Salvage what you can, girl. Not much on the market. A bird in hand and all."

They continued walking.

"I'm not concerned," Mel said. "Dave spent much of the last few months out of the country. We saw it as an opportunity to refresh our relationship."

"How long was he gone?"

Bitch, thought Mel. "Six or seven weeks, probably."

"Where's he living when he's here?"

"He'll be coming back home now that the traveling's normalized. We miss each other. Kind of like dating again."

Janet reached the gym door first and held it open. Mel glanced one last time toward the parking lot. Still no Dave. The sonuvabitch would probably use every spare second of the 30-minute grace period.

She felt her face turn hot and, undoubtedly, red.

"Margaritas later?" Janet asked.

"Thanks. That would be fun sometime, but Dave's coming. Date night after the game."

Janet flashed her eyebrows skeptically as Mel walked inside.

CHAPTER 25

Dave's Office
October 21, 3:58 p.m. Mountain Time

Followed closely by Brian Middleton and Jennifer, Dave walked down the corridor between the cubicles. His watch showed 3:58. Anne had stuck her head in the conference room door at precisely 3:55, and Dave wrapped things up in less than a minute, remarkable for him.

Unfortunately, Brian, his VP of engineering, did not understand some of the nuances of collaborating with another company, especially when your company was the little guy in the equation. He followed Dave from the meeting, pleading his case. Jennifer tagged along, prepared to defend her position.

"It's due diligence," Brian said. "We shouldn't just accept it blindly. What if they inadvertently did something that undermines our hardware's performance?"

Dave tapped his hand along the top of the cubicles they passed as they walked. "Think of them as an OEM," Dave said. "We're delivering our hardware. They're adding their code. It's done all the time."

"But they're delivering the firmware to us because it has to integrate with our firmware."

Brian and Jennifer followed Dave into his office.

"You're talking about hacking the Aldrich code," Dave said." How would you feel if they reverse engineered your code?"

"You're too trusting, Dave."

Jennifer started to say something, but Dave waved a flat hand at her as a signal to keep quiet. He sat down behind his desk, starting to pack his briefcase.

Brian sighed deeply and then spoke again. "How do we really know that the Aldrich isn't embedding something ugly in their code? They could be reading our code back and reverse engineering our stuff anyway."

"If that were the case, they could do that by simply purchasing our product and loading their code on top of it. You're not thinking clearly."

"I understand a normal buy-sell deal," Middleton said. "That's not what's going on here. The two systems rely on the integrity of one another. We're taking it on faith that the Aldrich engineers know what they're doing when it comes to our device. That's a huge leap when you consider that what we're doing has never been done before. So, we cannot really know how their code might be distorting the data. And there is no way to be certain that our output is accurate."

"You're paranoid, Brian," Jennifer said. "We have a thorough validation test for their code. If it identifies a certain genotype, we can be certain that it's accurate."

"Do you think our validation test is going to catch an event-triggered virus?"

Jennifer rolled her eyes. "Brian, they're our partners. If they sabotage the code, they're sabotaging themselves..."

"Excuse me, but you don't know what you're talking about. When you plow through all our code for 18 months like some of my guys have, then you can tell me what we should or shouldn't do."

"You can't mean that. I can write code backward faster than some of your guys can write it forward."

Dave looked at his watch. 4:03. The game started in less than half an hour. He had a five-minute walk to the car and a 25-minute drive. He could not afford to be late. He slapped his hands on his desk with a thunderous thud that echoed through the room. Jennifer and Brian shut up instantly.

"I don't want to hear anymore. I have a plane to catch and I'm already going to miss part of my daughter's volleyball game..."

"God, Dave," Jennifer said. "I am so sorry."

"You go," Brian said. "We'll work this out between us."

Dave looked at them both coldly. "I can see that," he said with a skeptical glare. "Wouldn't be wise to take that on faith. My guess is that we're discussing a moot point. Taking the ego out of it, Brian, how likely is it that your team can de-compile the Aldrich code under any circumstances?"

Brian bent forward, hands folded in his lap. He looked down at his hands.

"That's not a very hard question," Dave said.

"Not very likely, I suppose," Brian answered.

"Meant to piss Jenn off and remind her that she's an infiltrator from the Aldrich?"

"No, it's, well... It's a sincere effort."

"Really, Brian?" Dave said evenly. "And how about you, Jenn? Have you got your head so far up your ass that you'll believe this just to stay paranoid and prove yourself an outsider? How stupid do you two think I am?"

"We don't think you're stupid," Jennifer said.

As Jennifer scrambled, Brian said nothing. His nostrils flared. He had made it known that it bothered him that Dave, a sales and marketing guy by background, had never written any code. Dave knew that made him damn stupid in Brian's mind. More than once, Brian made it clear that he never understood why Hepp recruited him.

"Save it, Jenn," Dave said, now turning his fire back on Brian. "Brian, if you screw with the morale of our personnel one more time, you can kiss your big options payday good-bye."

Brian did not respond, his face tense. He stared at Dave but averted his eyes when Dave returned his glare. Picking up his briefcase, Dave rose from his chair and headed for the door.

"The two of you kiss and make up as soon as I get out of here. If I get word that your working relationship is not both constructive and professional while I'm gone, there will be hell to pay when I get back."

As he brushed past her, Jennifer gently grabbed Dave's arm and whispered, "Thanks."

Only more irritated by the gesture, Dave shook her off and headed out the door.

Arriving at his car, Dave reached into his pocket for his keys. Not finding them there, he searched his briefcase. Nothing. 4:17 on his watch. He saw his suitcase in the backseat. Anne had not returned his keys. He ran inside and up the front stairs. But he could not find Anne. Then from his office window, he saw her by his car, his keys dangling from her hand. He dashed back down the stairs finally meeting her in the lobby at 4:26.

"Sorry, Dave."

Dave struggled to catch his breath from the chase. He looked at her but did not have the energy or the heart to harangue her. He had done everything he could to be on time for the game. She had done everything she could to help him. He already felt like hell for showing emotion to Brian and Jennifer. Control meant being in control of his emotions as well.

"Not your fault," he said as he grabbed the keys. "I'll see you later."

"Have a safe trip," she called after him.

Screw the trip, he thought, but knew he would relegate that to wishful thinking.

4:28.

He turned the engine over. An orange LED shone by the gas gauge. He pressed a button on the dash.

The screen said, "18 miles to empty."

Eighteen miles to the high school. He gritted his teeth and tightened his grip on the wheel as he raced to the convenience store at the bottom of the hill.

He put the gas nozzle into the tank at 4:38. The credit card approval on the pump took an eternity. 4:40: "select your fuel…" He pressed the premium button and lifted the nozzle. Fill it up all the way or just enough to give him a decent cushion to get to the game? He might not have time after the game to add enough gas to get to the airport and back, especially since he planned to be moving well in excess of the speed limit. When the gas pump said eleven gallons, he released the handle.

4:48.

He pulled away, leaving the pump beeping with the receipt hanging out of its printer.

CHAPTER 26

Fort Collins High School
October 21, 5:17 p.m. Mountain Time

Mel twisted the roster in her hands. In the fifth game of the match, Fort Collins and Greeley North were tied at two games each, but Fort Collins now trailed 12-13 and rally scoring was in effect. Greeley North had the serve. Liv stood in Fort Collins' front row dead center.

Looking at her wrist, Mel saw that it was 5:13. Still no Dave.

The serve shot over the net in a line drive to Liv's right. Chelsea, Janet's daughter, dived for the ball and stuck a forearm in front of it just before it hit wood. The ball ricocheted back toward Liv, less than three feet from Chelsea. Liv instinctively threw a hand in front of her face, deflecting the ball. Stumbling back, Liv's eyes followed the ball as it soared high into the air over her head. Then she seemed disoriented, losing sight of the ball. Chelsea ran up in front of her to jump for the ball as it descended. Timing her leap perfectly, Chelsea spiked the ball into the midst of Greeley's defenders.

13-13. Tie game.

The serve now went to Fort Collins. Chelsea rotated back to serve.

As Liv shifted to the right side of the front row, she glanced toward Mel. Mel knew she was looking for Dave. As she silently cursed him one more time, Mel felt her phone vibrate in her jeans pocket. This had better be you, she thought as she pulled the phone out.

"Dave Clement," read the caller ID.

Balancing the phone in the palm of her hand, she pondered it for a few seconds. He would only tell her some story about another minor catastrophe at the office that justified his tardiness. She did not want to hear it. With the phone still vibrating, she put it back in her pocket.

"Let's go, Fort Collins!" she yelled, now rising from her seat as Chelsea nailed a beautiful line-drive serve that looked like it would smack wood right in the midst of the Greeley players. One of the Greeley girls reached out with an arm that seemed ten feet long, whacking the ball straight back over the net at Liv.

In the air as the ball shot over the net, Liv swung down hard with her right arm, sending the ball slamming into the ground on the Greeley side. The crowd erupted.

14-13, Fort Collins.

The phone began vibrating again. 5:15. "You lose, Dave," Mel mumbled to herself. She jumped to her feet cheering Liv's play.

Chelsea set to serve for game point. She lined this one right into the midst of Greeley's back row and the game ended.

15-13, Fort Collins.

The Fort Collins girls ran to each other and jumped around in a giant huddle. Breaking out into a single file line, they slapped hands with the Greeley girls who too had lined up single file.

Mel looked across to Janet and caught her eye. She gave her a big thumbs-up. Janet nodded, a wide grin overwhelming her proud face. Mel mouthed the word "Margaritas." Janet nodded approval.

As Mel walked down the bleachers to the floor, she glimpsed Dave striding in through the gym's main entrance. Seeing her, he waved and smiled. Then he slumped his shoulders and blew the air out to illustrate that he must have had a very tough afternoon. Once she thought that was cute, even adorable. Now it just stoked her resentment. If he would just acknowledge that he screwed up. Just once – instead of making up some excuse, pardoning himself one more time through the special dispensation of business burdens.

Just go away, Dave, she thought. Why even bother?

He came up and hugged her. She patted him perfunctorily on his nascent love handles and then pushed him gently away.

"I'm sorry I'm late," he said. "They just won't let me alone…"

Mel stared at him, mouth agape, her head shaking slowly from side to side. "Dave," she finally said over his blather. "Not now!"

He leaned toward her ear and whispered, "What are you bitching at me for? I did my best. I'm here, aren't I?"

She looked into his eyes, stood on her toes, and whispered back, "Screw you."

Dave flipped his palms skyward to say that he did not get the point. Mel felt no compunction to respond to his gesture. Instead, she walked quickly over to Liv and threw her arms around her.

"Great game, sweetheart!" she said.

"Mom, I'm sweaty," Liv said self-consciously as her mother squeezed her.

Mel waved to Chelsea and the other girls, calling out "great game" to each of them by name. Chelsea and two others came over for their hugs.

"My mom said she'll take a rain check on the margaritas," Chelsea whispered in Mel's ear.

"Tell her thanks."

Dave stood off to the side, ignored. Mel looked back to him. Liv followed her eyes. Seeing her Dad, she ran up to him.

"Thanks for coming, Daddy," she said, throwing her arms around him. "I've really missed you."

"But I just…"

"Got here?" she finished for him. "I know. That's okay. You tried."

Dave reciprocated the hug. At least Liv understood. Mel watched the interchange. She did not have to let him back in the house yet, but she could not deny Liv her father anymore.

"Still have time for dinner, big shot?" Mel asked rhetorically.

"You bet."

The three of them started walking toward the exit.

"You should have seen our daughter," Mel said. "She spiked one right there at the end that pretty much locked it up."

"It was just a great set-up, Mom. Almost anybody could have done that."

"I doubt that," Dave said.

"What about your three other points?" Mel asked.

Liv put an arm on each parent's shoulder. "It was great. This one girl for Greeley - "

A shrill sound rose from Dave's coat pocket. Mel and Liv looked at him, half-threatening.

"It can wait," he said, pressing a button on the side of the phone to stop the ring.

"Well, this girl from Greeley kept trash talkin' me under the net. She just made me want it more."

Dave unconsciously pulled the phone out and looked at the caller ID. He began to trail behind.

"You didn't look like you felt tired at all today," Mel said.

"The meds, I guess. Or adrenaline. I'm not -"

"What is it, Brian?" Dave said, the phone suddenly at his ear.

Liv stopped in mid-sentence. She looked back at her father, his head down, listening intently, totally re-absorbed in his own little world. Liv inhaled deeply and shook her head.

Grabbing Mel's arm, she drifted with her in the general direction of her car while Dave kept holding up the "just one minute" finger.

"We'll see you at the Charco Broiler," Mel said as she walked away from him rolling her eyes. It will be the last time, she thought.

CHAPTER 27

Fort Collins, Colorado – Charco Broiler Restaurant
October 21, 5:47 p.m. Mountain Time

Liv and Mel sat in a booth in the lighted back area of the otherwise dark restaurant. Smelling of grilled beef, the family-owned Fort Collins staple had great steaks, responsive service, and an Old West motif. The booths in the darkened area could be romantic, almost grotto-like with candlelight. Liv insisted they not sit there, although until her discovery of boys, she would typically insist on the family sitting in the dark where she would draw castles and princesses on the back of the kids menu.

Their drink order – three iced teas - arrived before Dave joined, the phone still attached to his ear. As he sat down, he put his index finger to his lips and then covered his open ear with his hand so he could hear better. Dutifully, mother and daughter stopped talking and opened their menus. After a moment of silence passed filled only with Dave's phone discussion of office politics with Jennifer Winters, Liv leaned forward.

"Daddy," she whispered.

He bounced a shushing index finger on his lips. Liv did not take this instruction.

"Daddy," she persisted. "You'll get brain cancer."

Mel laughed, but Dave just kept going.

"It's in your hands, Jennifer. Brian's call to me sounded genuinely apologetic. Give him a chance. He's a bright guy... All right... All right... I've gotta go... I'll be late for my plane... Okay, see ya next week... We'll talk."

He pressed the "end" button on his phone.

Mel glared at him. "What plane?"

"I forgot that I had a trip to Geneva tonight."

"You forgot an international trip? Either you have Alzheimer's or you think I'm an idiot."

"As odd as it sounds, I completely forgot about it. Anne calls it divorce dementia."

"You're not divorced," Liv said.

"And I never want to be," he responded.

"Then it can't be that important," Mel said. "Delay it."

"I can't. This is a must-attend meeting at the World Health Organization in Geneva." He paused for effect, but Mel and Liv remained non-plussed. "Do you want me to give everything up?" he asked. "If that's what it takes to get this family back together, I'll do it."

"Good," Mel said. "Then don't go to Geneva."

Dave knitted his eyebrows. "But... I have commitments, a moral obligation. Unless I formally resign my position, I can't just walk away from what has to be done."

"So you really don't mean you would give everything up to get this family back together," she said. "What time's your flight?" She picked up a pink sweetener packet, shaking it violently before ripping it open and pouring it into her iced tea.

"8:40."

"Fort Collins?"

"No, I'm skipping the commuter and driving to DIA. Gives me more time with you. I don't have to be on the road 'til 6:30."

She looked at her watch, her face red. 5:58. "Half an hour," she said. "I don't know why I thought you'd change."

"I'm doing what I have to do," he said. "And because of it, I have news."

"We can talk about it after we order. We don't have that much time if you're going to make your flight."

"I'm ready," Dave said after quickly glancing at the menu.

"So tell me about the game," Dave said to Liv. "What did the coach say?"

"We left right away, Daddy," she responded, a get-a-clue look crossing her face.

"Well, what do you think he'll say?"

"I think he'll be happy. Like really happy. Greeley North beat us badly twice last year. And only one of their starters graduated. We were just that much better today."

"You're a big part of that difference," Mel said.

"It helps that I feel better."

"So you have this thing under control, sweetheart?" Dave asked.

"Think so. Some good days and some not-so-good, but all in all - "

Dave saw the waiter passing by and called to him. "Excuse me, but we need to order and eat pretty fast. I have a plane to catch."

"Yes, sir. I'll be back as soon as I deliver these drinks."

"We can order right now. We know exactly what we want."

"Daddy, I don't."

"We've been here a hundred times. You can figure it out while I order. Get the southwestern chicken. That's always good."

Liv looked toward her mother and rolled her eyes.

"She was counting on a steak," Mel said.

The waiter gave Dave his own "just one minute" finger as he gave the drinks to the people at the next table. In silence, Liv and Mel quickly searched their menus. Dave kept glancing impatiently toward the waiter until he finally returned.

"Yes, sir?" the waiter said as he flipped open his order book.. A senior at the high school, he recognized Liv and whispered a shy "hello." Liv smiled back.

Each family member ordered. As soon as the waiter collected the menus, Dave spoke, "What a day. I didn't think I'd ever get out. We had a major issue with the firmware. Now, I can't believe I have to get on another plane. I really just want to spend time with you guys."

Liv snorted as she answered, "I'll believe that when I see it."

"Honey, I tried to make the game. I can't help that I got caught at the office. It's certainly not because I like it. I do it for us. So we can live like we do. And maybe better eventually."

"I'm happy with the way things are, Daddy. We have everything we need. Except you're not living at home anymore. Even when you did, you were never around."

Liv leaned into Mel for a hug. Mel raised her eyebrows at Dave.

"The waiter's cute," Liv whispered to her mom.

"What are you two talking about?" Dave interrupted.

"Girl talk, Daddy."

"Since I'm leaving soon, can I be included?"

"In girl talk?" Liv asked.

"His feelings are hurt," Mel said, grinning.

"My feelings aren't hurt."

"That's okay," Liv said. "You can talk girl talk. What did you think of the waiter?"

Dave blushed. "Young," he finally said. "And you're way too young."

"Daddy, where have you been? Like, I am one of the few girls I know who has never even been kissed."

Dave nodded and paused to squeeze lemon in his tea before responding. "What does the doctor say?" he asked.

"My count's 520," Liv said matter-of-factly. She leaned over the table and sipped through the straw of her Coke. "That's good news."

She sat up and let the carbonation tickle her throat. She suppressed a belch, placing a hand over her mouth. Impishly, she glanced at her dad. "Sorry," she said.

"No problem. Enjoy. It's good to see you relax."

"Have to keep the count up or I wouldn't be playing volleyball."

"Is that what the specialist said?"

"Pretty much. It's really up to Mom and me. If I go much below 500, my immune system gets too weak to fight off sicknesses. That's when I'm not supposed to overdo it."

"At all," Mel added.

"I gather you guys have debated this one."

"We understand each other now, don't we, Liv?"

"Yes, mother." Liv leaned into her straw again.

Dave turned to Mel. "What's her count been doing?"

"Holding steady last week. The latest meds bumped her up right away, but they came down a little and then leveled off. Jury's still out."

Mel glanced at Liv who held the Coke glass in one hand, the straw in the other, her lips puckered around the plastic. She looked wide-eyed at her parents, following their conversation.

"Doc Resnick thinks she'll be fine if she takes her pills when she's supposed to."

"So we're in maintenance mode?"

Mel blanched at the use of the word "we."

"Right, Dave. We are in maintenance mode." She put emphasis on the "we."

"It should be we. I should be home."

"Not yet."

"Yet? So when?"

Mel sipped her tea. "So what's your news?" she asked, ignoring his question. "About Liv."

He looked back and forth between his wife and daughter. "It may be very good news. One of the drug developers I work with contacted me this morning. She knows of a new experimental approach that will not only raise Liv's count, but kill her HIV."

"Omigod, Daddy!" Liv said, rising out of her seat. But Mel placed a hand on her shoulder and gently guided her back down.

"A cure, Dave?" she asked. "How does she know it works?"

He folded his hands on the table and looked at them for a moment before looking up. "She's one of the best scientists I know. I trust her."

"Is this her discovery?"

"I don't know. I'm meeting with her for the details next week."

"So you don't know if it works?"

"She wouldn't say it did if it didn't," he replied. "She did say it's complicated so there must be some hoops to go through."

"Who is she?" Liv asked.

"I can't say, honey. It's all very hush-hush. I'm not even supposed to know."

Liv took her mother's hand. Mel pulled her closer and hugged her.

"It could be pretty wonderful," Mel said. "But we're not going to get too excited yet."

"Look, I don't know what she meant by complicated," Dave said. "But I believe this scientist is on to something very real. It's more hope than we had yesterday."

Mel studied him before leaning across the table and giving him a quick kiss on the lips. He smiled.

Liv came around the table and hugged him. "Thank you, Daddy."

"Just keep praying," he said, reciprocating the hug.

"Always," she said.

"So you never told us how Africa went?" Mel asked as Liv returned to her seat.

"Which countries did you see, Dad?" asked Liv even though she already knew the answer.

"Nigeria and Sierra Leone."

"Why, Dave? There's news of war in Nigeria every day."

"Well, I don't plan to go back soon. It was horrifying."

The waiter returned, interrupting. "Sir, the kitchen is backed up. Your steak will be 20 minutes."

"20 minutes? That won't work. I have a plane to catch."

"I apologize, but it can't be much faster than that."

Dave breathed in deeply through his nose before speaking. "What can you do quickly?" he asked.

"We can get a steak sandwich pretty fast. It's a thinner cut and we keep them on the grill."

"Make it a steak sandwich then. I'll just take it with me when I go."

Mel and Liv shared a glance of exasperation.

"Will everyone want a sandwich to go then?" the waiter asked.

"No," asserted Mel. "The two of us will stay and enjoy our meal."

"I'm sorry," Dave said after the waiter left. "I can't afford to miss this flight. Evan Conger's meeting me at the airport. I can't let him down."

Mel shrugged her shoulders. Liv curled up close to her in the booth. Liv popped up suddenly and picked up her iced tea.

"A toast to Dad and his secret drug lab," she said.

Her parents smiled and the three clinked glasses.

CHAPTER 28

Clement Home
October 21, 9:45 p.m. Mountain Time

Mel reached into her bedroom closet for a white robe.

"Oh, no!" came a cry from the hall bath.

"Liv, what's wrong?" Mel asked as she hurried to the bathroom.

Liv's hands covered her face in front of the mirror. "It's back," she said, a tear trickling down her face as she opened her hands and let her mother see her.

"Look," she said, panic in her voice. "It's starting. I overdid it."

"You've had them before. They're not a sign of anything."

Mel looked in the mirror over Liv's shoulder, barely detecting a small bump forming on her lip.

"You can't even see it," Mel said. She left the room and returned a moment later with a 400-milligram acyclovir tablet.

"This will stop it," she said.

Liv swallowed the capsule and returned to administering Clearasil to a handful of nearly imperceptible blemishes on her face. A few minutes later, she crawled under the covers of her bed.

Mel entered her room and leaned over to kiss her goodnight. Liv's forehead felt hot to her lips. "You feeling okay, sweetie?" she asked.

"Just tired." She kicked the covers off as Mel started to leave the room.

"You'll be cold."

"Mom, I'm hot."

Mel walked down the hall to her bathroom medicine chest and pulled out a thermometer. Damned volleyball, she thought. She should have put her foot down and not let her play until the count was higher.

But she needed to keep Liv's morale up. And her own. Maybe she needed a sense of normalcy. As it turned out, throwing Dave out had not helped that cause.

She returned to Liv's room. Liv hurriedly shoved something under the pillow.

"What's that?"

"My diary."

"I won't read your diary."

"Still - "

"I don't know why you don't do a blog like every other teenager. Then I could go online to see what's going on." Mel smiled and held Liv's gaze.

"That's exactly why not, mother."

Mel put the thermometer in Liv's mouth. A moment later, it beeped.

"Normal, right?" Liv asked as soon as Mel pulled the plastic stick from her mouth.

"99.4. Slight fever." Mel spoke evenly, repressing the jolt of alarm she felt in her stomach.

"That's minor," Liv said.

Mel caressed her forehead. "It is. You've just overdone things a bit. Your body's asking you to slow down."

"How? I have volleyball, two pre-AP courses, choir, church group. And two or three other things I'm forgetting."

"Very funny, smart-alec. We just need to figure out a way to get you more down time. You're not like the other kids anymore."

"Not what I want to hear, Mom. Anyway, down time and I are opposites. Hopefully, Dad's friend really has a cure. That will fix everything once and for all."

"Me, too." Placing her hand in her daughter's, Mel thought of Dave, by now in the air somewhere over the Midwest. Dave's assistant Anne, who kept Mel in the loop throughout the separation, had faxed his itinerary to her after Mel called on the way home from what turned out to be a delicious mother-daughter meal at the Charco Broiler.

"Sometimes you're just like your father, sweetheart."

"I'm not sure how to take that."

"It's a compliment... mostly," Mel said, a melancholy smile on her face. "He really does love you."

"I think he loves his job more, Mom."

Mel pondered this comment for a moment. "No, he doesn't love his job at all. I think he's afraid of it. He's afraid to turn his back on it. That's why he never lets go."

"What's he afraid of?"

"Failure. Afraid he'll lose the job and let us down. He's lost jobs before. There's no loyalty in the corporate world."

Liv adjusted her position in the bed and rolled over on her side, facing Mel. Her voice took on a sincere little-girl tone.

"Mom, how can we make him afraid of losing us instead?"

CHAPTER 29

36,000 feet over the North Atlantic
October 22, 4:15 a.m. Atlantic Time

Evan Conger listened to the engines. Their persistent hum sounded normal. Halifax lay only 25 minutes southwest. The pilots said the control tower there had cleared them for an emergency landing. They would be back on the ground within half an hour.

Evan's knuckles whitened from their tight grip on the arm rests. The curled-up woman beside him stared catatonically out the window. After the first few minutes of nervous chatter following the pilot's announcement about the course reversal, the passengers grew very quiet. In the silent anticipation, every thudding collision with turbulent air, every crinkle of metal, and every pitch change in the engines reverberated in the cabin. The hum of the ailerons shifting position reassured; they still worked.

I ran to catch this flight, Evan thought. Bad decision, he concluded as he caught a whiff of burnt wires. Should have lingered in Boulder a little longer.

He had planned to walk from his seat in business class back to coach class to let Dave Clement know he made the flight, but turbulence and meal service had kept everyone in their seats for hours. And now this. Dave probably understood that he did not deliberately miss their appointment in the Admiral's Club; the man traveled enough himself to know that schedules could get very tight. Evan had simply texted "Delayed" and Dave responded "Ok." They would cover the details when they met face to face.

In the meantime, he used the flight time to finally read more than the chilling summary from Sheila's flash drive. Sheila had converted most of the information to pdf files. Evan had uploaded them to his smartphone via bluetooth from his laptop. He thought about uploading them to a cloud repository, but thought the information far too sensitive to leave out in the open on strange servers. The NSA or other interested parties could easily access it.

As he suspected, Claire had shown him only what she wanted him to see at her offices. If Sheila's info gave him accurate data, he had to stop Claire and her team.

When they got on the ground, he would brief Dave. Sheila's notes confided that Liv Clement had HIV. Evan still had to do more digging, but Sheila suggested that the girl's unexplained HIV might in some twisted way be correlated to the Aldrich. If it did, Evan thought he could help Sheila fix that situation.

And the Prodeus PDNAs played a critical part in the Aldrich plan. Dave could help him get to the bottom of that. When Dave learned what Sheila had to say, he would be highly motivated.

The turbulence settled. The lights of the Nova Scotia coast appeared below. Evan relaxed his grip on the armrests. He withdrew the packet of faxed handwritten notes from the seatback pocket. The fax from Warren Sturbridge, a friend on a six-month assignment with Doctors Without Borders in Sierra Leone, gave further credence to the information that Sheila had slipped him.

Two rows up, Conger's deputy at WHO – the real operational brains of drug deployment, Conger always said – turned back to look at him. He wondered if he should bring her into the loop on the fax and the Aldrich activities. She smiled when she caught his eye. Simultaneously, they shrugged their shoulders, both acknowledging the irony of their airport sprint now that the plane had turned around.

A startled flight attendant gasped loudly. Through the open curtain to first class, Evan saw her standing just outside the secured cockpit door. Black smoke leached through its seals into the passenger cabin. She pressed a combination of buttons and opened the door. Smoke and the splash of a spotlight poured out. The explosive gush of a fire extinguisher sounded amidst the shouts of the crew and terrified passengers.

The pilot came on the PA. "Calm down back there," he said. "We're okay. Just a little smoky."

Mumbles of "shut up," "what did he say," and shouts of "quiet" filled the cabin.

The pilot continued, "It looks much worse than it is. Looks like a little wiring issue. That's why they equip the cockpit with a couple oversized fire extinguishers. We've been trained for this. I can guarantee, however, that the ride will get a lot bumpier. Nothing to be worried about. Please stay belted in your seats. We'll be dropping below 12,000 feet. Very rapidly. That's going to feel like an e-ticket roller coaster descent, but this baby's meant to take that kind of abuse. Once we get down there, we'll crack open our cockpit windows and clear the air a bit."

Immediately, the clunking of ailerons could be heard. Next came the high-pitched squeal of the engines as the plane bent forward into a dive. Evan watched as the flight attendant that had opened the cabin door flung herself into a jump seat, hurriedly belting up.

Evan reached into the seat pocket for his phone. Its waterproof, solar powered case had proven useful insurance for WHO teams deployed in extreme and remote climates. Choking down the fear rising in his gut, he leaned the thick case against the binder he had been reviewing in his lap. He checked for wi-fi, but there was none, probably damaged by the wiring problem. His fingers hesitated over the tiny keypad on the screen. He appreciated the pilot's calm, but cockpit fires had a bad track record; he had reviewed data on them as surgeon general.

He could write a note to his wife Michelle. Or he could try to save a lot of lives, maybe millions if the Aldrich ended up rolling out its plan across all of sub-Saharan African.

He looked out the window. In the darkness, he no longer saw lights; where did the land go? He briefly prayed that they at least made land, providing better odds for the phone being found. He found it hard to breathe as the smoke slowly thickened in the cabin. He looked down at the small backlit screen, and his thumbs began quickly dancing across the tiny keys.

Michelle, forgive me, he thought.

A moment later, Evan struggled to concentrate on the keyboard as G-forces thrust him back against his seat. The high-pitched whining of the engines suddenly blocked out all other noise as they plunged downward through the sky.

CHAPTER 30

Clement Home
October 22, 2:05 a.m. Mountain Time

Mel rolled over in bed, switching pillows for a cooler one from Dave's side of the bed.

Worried about Liv and worried about Dave, she could not keep her eyes closed. She stared at the ceiling. She could thoroughly dislike him at times, but she could never stop loving him. Since the outset of their marriage, his travel had made her an insomniac. International travel made her particularly apprehensive, all the more so since September 11, 2001.

Dave did not know she only slept well with him lying beside her. If he did, he would have the upper hand in this round of poker she had dealt. Damn, I'm good, she thought. But lonely and unable to sleep.

"I hope it's worth it," she said aloud.

The white digital read-out on the cable box said 2:05. She grabbed the remote from the nightstand. *Modern Family.* She wondered how many reruns it had in the can. She pressed the button and surfed for something more interesting to her tonight. She rolled through the channels, passing CNN twice before she paused the remote long enough to see what all the red lights and commotion were about. A talking head stood in the darkness with the flashing lights from emergency vehicles reflecting in the dark water off the pier behind him. The tag-line in white letters on the bottom of the screen said: "Peggy's Cove, Nova Scotia."

She pressed the volume button. The instant she recognized the flight number, she picked up the landline and dialed Dave's mobile. When she got his voicemail, she slowly placed the phone on the bed – and sobbed.

CHAPTER 31

Cameron Pass, Aldrich Mountain Lab
October 22, 2:42 a.m. Mountain Time

The ethereal glow from the computer screen distorted Eldridge Perry's facial features in the darkness. He moved his mouse back over the video window and replayed the CNN clip from Nova Scotia.

"Anderson, authorities here tell us off the record that this is a recovery operation, not a rescue operation. That means they expect to find no survivors. Helping to support that, local fishermen told me the plane appeared to break up before impacting the water. That may indicate a bomb of some kind is involved, but as we've seen time and time again, these investigations often take months..."

Eldridge held the mouse pointer over the pause button and clicked. The room instantly went silent, the low electronic hum of the computer now the only sound.

He let go of the mouse and rubbed his hands slowly back and forth along the arms of his chair. Eldridge thought that Mike Farley, Claire's new security chief, amounted to nothing more than a thug. He warned Claire that Farley's crude methods, honed on the streets of Northern Ireland, could backfire on them. Eldridge believed tactics should be patiently deployed as in a chess game, not like a rugby scrum.

"Sloppy work," he mumbled. "Sloppy damned work."

His phone rang. Caller ID showed it was Claire.

"You got what you wanted," he answered.

"Don't pout, Eldridge," she said. "It's a big win."

"A bit extreme," he said.

"Sometimes extreme is needed. And we're not finished. There are still more bad guys out there. We knew we'd face this in some form and we handled it. We'll keep handling it. Are you with me?"

"Of course," he said. "I think some of the tactics are too risky, but I understand the math of trading off a handful of lives for many."

"I hope so," she said. "I don't think you or anyone else can now doubt just how committed and unwavering we need to be."

After she hung up, he thought about how things could yet go wrong. He opened a new window on the screen. He studied his "chess pieces" and pondered moves yet available. With Mike Farley on Claire's payroll, Eldridge needed backup plans, insurance policies. He dragged his mouse across the screen, paused at Dave Clement's name. Claire had anointed the gifted Clement to ultimately replace the sickly Hepp as CEO at Prodeus. Eldridge had strongly agreed with the choice initially. More and more in the last year, he had developed doubts. Not doubts about Clement's skills. They were world class. But Dave did not seem ready to play well with others. He seemed to have an overdeveloped sense of right and wrong. So he and Claire zeroed in on Dave's vulnerabilities, and finally one in particular – the perfect insurance policy with a family man. He moved his mouse again, highlighting two words:

Liv Clement

For the moment, at least, that chess piece sat on exactly the right square. Poor kid, he thought. A principled, loving father looked good in the movies, but, in Liv's case, that amounted to a major liability. Her future did not look bright.

"Helluva birthright," he uttered into the darkness.

Public Offerings continues in

Public Offerings Book Two: The Price of a Life

Enjoy the free excerpt that follows

Learn more at www.PublicOfferings.net

Follow at www.Facebook.com/PublicOfferings

EXCERPT:

PUBLIC OFFERINGS BOOK TWO:

THE PRICE OF A LIFE

CHAPTER 1

Southeastern Sierra Leone, Kono District
October 22, 10:15 am GMT

His stethoscope hung around his neck as a matter of habit, offering the only visible clue that Warren Sturbridge, close friend and protégé of Evan Conger, practiced medicine. He walked up the narrow path, thick grass over six feet tall brushing at his sides, his twenty-something companion a half-step behind. After five months in Sierra Leone, Sturbridge learned from the locals to walk at a much easier pace than he did when he first arrived from San Diego. The soaking humidity and tropical sun ensured he remembered the lesson.

"When your laptop disappeared, I thought we would never get the report finished," said Tom Czerski, a short but lean man now, just over a year into his two-year Peace Corps tour.

"I told you to have faith," said Sturbridge, a week's worth of gray and black stubble on his face. "Pen and paper may be slow, but it's very reliable."

The men walked carefully around a small bomb crater in the trail, knowing that craters provided excellent cover for booby traps. While peace had been officially declared, the real experience on the ground, particularly outside the main cities, displayed a balkanized array of competing militias and stragglers who knew only violence as a means to achieve their ends. Booby traps, landmines, checkpoints, ambush, and intimidation remained the norm in the bush.

Sturbridge had arrived in the country with a decent paunch on his belt. That had been gone for months and his legs, arms and abs had begun to show definition that he looked forward to proudly showing off to his wife upon his return home. He viewed the overall experience as very invigorating but missed his wife and his two-year-old son – and hot showers.

"The World Bank guy – Adrian Guerra – must think you have a good chance of getting the funds," Czerski said.

"Why? Because Adrian volunteered his office to type the report?" Sturbridge replied.

"Do you think he'd waste his time?"

"No. No, I guess not. Something about the guy just sets off my alarm bells." Hearing movement in the tall grass, the doctor held a hand up and both men stopped, holding their breath as they listened.

"What is it?" Czerski asked.

"Bird probably," the doctor responded as he wiped his already damp shirt against the side of his face to stop the trickle of an irritating drop of sweat. He listened for further sounds but heard nothing else out of the ordinary. After thirty seconds, he nodded at the volunteer and they continued walking.

"Will Adrian or his World Bank team e-mail a copy of the finished product back to the Salk Institute?" Czerski asked.

"Not until I proofread it," Sturbridge said. "The copy I asked them to type is a photocopy of the handwritten version I faxed to Dr. Conger a few days ago. Evan knows me well enough that I don't mind him catching a few grammatical errors. The important thing is that we've identified the HIV type here."

Thunder rumbled in the distance, a common rainy season event. The season would be over in a few months, but Sturbridge would be gone by then, so he might never know Sierra Leone without rain and mud.

"Will people be surprised that it's the same type as there is throughout the rest of the region?" Czerski quizzed, his breath starting to catch as the trail inclined upward steeply.

"Some will be. There are a few scientists that want new mutations to show up because they believe new variations could be more aggressive with shorter incubation periods. Shorter incubation periods could offer new pathways to cures and vaccines."

"Do you agree?" the Peace Corps volunteer asked.

"No. It's wishful thinking. The consistency we've discovered is good news. A little bit of stability gives us a better shot at beating this damned scourge. At least for a while."

"From the conversation I overheard with you and Adrian, he's definitely not in your camp on that."

"No, he's not."

The air turned green as the sun went behind the first of the rapidly advancing thunderheads. Sturbridge could almost taste the rain.

He had rushed the handwritten copy of his research in hopes that Evan Conger would present the key findings at the WHO conference that week. Adrian Guerra wanted to believe that Sierra Leone and other areas of West Africa had a different and more aggressive HIV type. Sturbridge concluded that was not the case, but Guerra stubbornly and inexplicably insisted the doctor was wrong.

Big drops of rain began falling and lightning struck with a crackling roar nearby.

"Doctor!" A voice called to Sturbridge and Czerski through sheets of rain that suddenly began blowing across their path. They hurried up the trail, arriving quickly at a large clearing.

"Doctor! Over here."

They entered the clearing and saw the man standing 30 yards off the path to the right. Sturbridge recognized him as one of the Leonean clerks from Adrian Guerra's World Bank office.

"What are you doing out here?" the doctor shouted over the rain.

The man waved a pile of paper at the men. "You know what this is?" the clerk called.

Sturbridge stopped in his tracks. It looked like his handwritten report. And it was getting drenched. "Is that my report?" he demanded.

"Yes, it is," the man yelled, an insane grin on his face.

"Why are you here with it? Is it finished? Have you typed it?"

"No, doctor. It's not finished. You must come see it."

Sturbridge looked at Czerski. The men shared a look that said, "What the hell…"

"Thank God you faxed one to Dr. Conger," Czerski said.

"We're going to get the original back right now," the doctor said.

With Sturbridge in the lead, they veered off the path and ran across the soppy clearing toward the clerk. As they closed the gap to about 15 yards, the clerk turned and raced into the brush behind him.

"Where are you going?" shouted the doctor. No good could come of this, he thought. He chastised himself for trusting Guerra.

They picked up their pace, the doctor staying just ahead of Czerski. Sturbridge felt the slight tension of the wire against his shin as it snapped from his momentum. He had cared for many victims of similar booby traps over the preceding months. He knew the odds. He turned wide-eyed to his young protégé whose wet face mirrored the terror on his own just before the bright, white flash of the explosion.

CHAPTER 2

Chicago - O'Hare Airport Admiral's Club
October 22 - 5:02 am Central Time

Drawn by the addictive aroma of fresh coffee, a bleary-eyed Dave Clement pushed the espresso machine's cappuccino button. As he watched the foamy liquid fill his cup, he wondered if the energy from the caffeine would trump the sleepiness the milky forth could induce. While he waited for the pour to finish, he straightened his shirt collar and smoothed the seam in his slacks. His clothes had not held up well during a long, restless night in a lounge chair in the Admirals Club. He could barely walk, let alone think.

He looked at the wall clock. 5:02 a.m. He had only a few minutes until he needed to go to the concourse for his flight to New York. Once in the Big Apple, he would take a cab from LaGuardia to JFK and catch a flight to Paris. From there, he would finally connect to Geneva on Air France. He would arrive in Switzerland at 8:30 in the morning, two days separated from a bed, a good night's sleep and a shower. Definitely an ordeal, but he would end up missing only the conference's opening cocktail reception. He hoped he would catch enough sleep en route to keep him awake for the meetings and sessions which he would start as soon as he arrived from the airport. Damned security line at DIA had been backed up at 7:40 the night before. Even with the long line, he would have been on time if TSA had not randomly pulled him out of line for a selective hand check. For some unexplained reason, they singled him out. First time in a decade for him. Only God knows why, he thought.

Once clear of the checkpoint, he flew down the escalator and caught a train right away. Five more minutes and he would have been on the flight to London and talking with Evan. Five more minutes would have saved him twelve hours of extra travel time. Instead, he spent the next hour finding a flight combination that would get him to Geneva as closely as possible to his missed connection. That put him on United to Chicago, connecting to American.

Four flights instead of two. On the bright side, it was good for extra frequent flyer segments to maintain his elite status. Nonetheless, the torture started immediately with a middle seat against the bathrooms in the back of coach flying out of Denver; the armrests seemed narrower than his hips. He had not been able to get international business class out of Chicago, but at least he had an aisle and American had some legroom in coach, especially on the triple 7.

When he arrived in Chicago, he reached for his phone to call Mel. Just like he always did when he traveled. The phone's LED readout told him it was 11:50 in Chicago, making it 10:50 in Fort Collins. Too late to call Mel without waking her. He had already pushed his luck with her earlier in the day. If he woke her, it would be a backward move, not a forward one. Instead, he called her mobile phone, figuring it would be turned off as per her habit, reposing in its charger for the night.

"Hi, Mel," he said to her voice mail. "Just wanted to tell you how great it was to be with you and Liv again. I know I rushed out tonight, but I hope you know my intentions were good..."

She won't buy that, he thought. He tried again. "I'm in Chicago. Trying to sleep on a chair in the Admirals Club. Missed my flight out of Denver so I have kind of an ordeal now to make my meeting in Geneva tomorrow. Spending time with you was definitely worth it. The people in Geneva will just have to understand that there's nothing more important than my family. I love you. Very much. With all my heart. Tell Liv the same, please. Bye. Love you. Love you both."

He pressed a button. That sounds manipulative, he thought. Very manipulative. He went through the prompts and canceled the message.

Shoving the phone back in his jacket pocket, he pondered taking an early morning flight back to Denver. With the time difference, he could be there by 8:30 in the morning. Not a good idea, he thought. Not yet. An hour later, the pings from texts with flight status woke him up as he finally dozed off. Irritated and groggy, he powered off his phone and nodded off again,

Now, five hours later, he finished his cappuccino and reached down for the handle on his rolling bag. With his free hand, he pulled his phone out of his pocket, discovering it was still turned off. He powered it on and headed for his plane. Waiting for the elevator to the concourse, he saw he had a voicemail from Mel. As he pressed the button to hear it, he glimpsed Fox News on a monitor to the left of the elevators. He picked up the words "airline disaster" on the marquis running along the bottom of the screen. He stepped toward the television, looking for a volume control.

"Can I help you, sir?" called a woman behind the reception desk.

"I can't hear it."

She aimed a remote past Dave, but the station cut to commercial.

"It said airline disaster," he said. "Do you know what happened?"

The voicemail started its playback in his ear: "Dave, I don't care what time you get this. Please call me. I need to know you're okay. I love you. I'm so sorry for everything."

"Doesn't look good," the receptionist answered. "Flight went down off Nova Scotia."

Dave glanced at the list of voicemails on his phone. There were six more from Mel, the last one only twenty minutes earlier.

"Canadian flight?" he asked the receptionist.

"Flight out of Denver bound for London," she said.

The handle of the rolling bag slipped out of Dave's fingers, banging off the floor.

CHAPTER 3

Fort Collins, Colorado; Silver Grille Cafe
October 22, 9:55 a.m. Mountain Time

Five hours later, Dave sat with Mel in a booth at the Silver Grille Café in downtown Fort Collins. He ordered eggs over easy and corned beef hash with a side of cinnamon toast, buttered and grilled slices of the restaurant's enormous cinnamon buns whose sweet and spicy aroma permeated the dining area. For once, Mel did not challenge him for ordering too much.

He sipped his coffee and adjusted his cup back in the saucer. Mel reached around it to take his hand in hers.

"I love you," she said.

"I love you, too. More than ever. I'm blessed to have you in my life."

Mel tilted her head and narrowed her eyes. He knew she was not accustomed to that kind of language from him.

"God spared me, Mel," he said.

"I'll say. God and the fact that the TSA pulled you out of the security line."

"For sure. If they don't do that, I'm on that flight. First time I've been pulled out in a decade probably. What are the odds? That's the good Lord looking out for me."

Mel nodded and squeezed his hand in both of hers. "It's time you came home."

He felt tears well up in his eyes. He had waited months for her to say that. He looked toward the wall and tried to wipe away the first traces with his fingers, but the feeling was too strong and a handful of tears made it over his cheeks and down to his jawline.

"I'm sorry," he mumbled.

"For tears?" she asked, her own tears now glistening below her eyes. "Don't be silly. If we can't cry a little about this, we don't, ah, we don't…"

She sobbed once and then inhaled deeply to stop herself from continuing.

He wanted desperately to go home with her. But he had deliberately asked her to meet him here first for breakfast after she dropped Liv at school. He knew if he drove directly home from the airport, he would find it almost impossible to do what he was about to do. He took both her hands now and looked directly into her eyes.

"I want to move back home more than anything. I know that I've made you and Liv secondary to my work. It's been misguided. I want to do better."

"It's okay. I understand. You obsess with your work because you worry about taking care of us. I know that. Before Liv came along and we had responsibilities, you knew how to relax. I just want that Dave back, the one I married."

"That Dave may never come back," he said. "In the moments after I saw the news about the plane, when I realized that Evan and his team were gone, something came to me. Something very insistent. And I can't let it go. I'm called to see this through in the business, to be more focused than ever. It's what I'm meant to do."

Mel let go of his hands and sat back, her mouth slightly agape. "I don't understand," she said.

"If I come home now, I won't be what I need to be at home. I'll disappoint you again."

"What?"

"I've been spared for a reason."

"Omigod, Dave. Don't do this."

"I'm serious. God wants me to have faith and double down on the vaccine effort. I don't know why, but I think it has something to do with finding a cure for Liv."

Mel's eyes blazed. "So you're not coming home? You're going to get on more airplanes? You're going to leave us to worry about you?"

"At least for a few weeks. I need to focus on the vaccine project. And I don't want to bring home the same workaholic problem that caused you to lock me out in the first place."

She leaned back in her seat and studied him. "You're not looking at this the right way, Dave. You've been spared to come home and be with us. Not to run around the world trying to be a hero."

"I only wish that's all it was."

"What the hell is wrong with you?"

"It's bigger than me."

"Bigger than us?"

He bit the inside of his cheek thoughtfully before answering. "I think so."

"So you're the damned second-coming now? It wasn't enough to think you were the savior of this family. You have to save the world. You need psychiatric help."

It surprised Dave that he remained peaceful both inside and out. "I truly love you, Mel. And I love Liv. More than anything in this world."

"Then come home. You're not the only one who got a second chance. We all did."

"I'd like nothing more, but it's too soon. You wouldn't be happy with me. For a while, I'm going to be gone more than ever, working harder than ever. Sorting out..."

"Why God spared you," she said, finishing for him. "And because you're big-time Dave Clement, the reason has to be earth-shaking. World class, right?"

"You don't believe me? You think it was just random that I missed that plane?"

Mel covered her eyes with her hands. She took a few deep breaths, working on perspective. "Listen, my love…"

When Mel said "my love" to him, she always meant it in the most condescending sense.

"…even if you did benefit from some cosmic intervention. I'd like to think that God appreciates the simple things, too – that His intervention isn't just reserved for world issues. And, if it is in this case, maybe it's about being home for your daughter, helping her grow up to be President or some other thing that meets your ego requirements."

He reached for her hands again, but she folded her arms in response.

"You are the most wonderful gift God ever gave me," he said. "I don't consider that a simple thing, but it's not a world issue. God does care about the day-to-day things. You're absolutely right. Fortunately or unfortunately, I know he wants me to do something that does not seem to fit our family plan. That knowledge is deep inside me, right at the core. For once, I need to be obedient."

She wiped the back of a hand across her eyes, her make-up streaked and eyes black from mascara. She tried again. "What about Liv's health? She needs an involved father."

"I think that's part of what I'll be doing. Conger was very involved in HIV management."

"That's not the same thing as being at home for her. She needs you to be a father first, not a champion."

He could feel a slight tear in the fabric of his resolve. He knew, though, that if he went home, he would quickly lose sight of the big picture and be drawn right back into the place where he most wanted to be.

Mel stared through him, shaking her head. Then she carefully folded her white cloth napkin and laid it on the table. She stood up. "You're breaking your daughter's heart."

"I'm trying to protect her."

Mel turned and walked away. He did not follow. He knew there was no point. He had let her down again. The clever idea of not yet going home seemed a lot less appealing than it did in the middle of the night at O'Hare International. He picked up the coffee cup and brought it to his lips, but did not drink. He put it back down and just stared into the black liquid.

"What the hell am I doing?" he mumbled.

CHAPTER 4

Loveland, Colorado: Prodeus Offices
October 26, 2:58 a.m. Mountain Time

Her facial features shrouded in shadows from the computer screen's blue light, Jennifer maneuvered her mouse in the darkness. To avoid discovery, she relied only on the screen's reflected light. The digital clock in the lower right hand corner of the screen said 2:58 a.m.

With the mouse, she pointed the arrow on the screen at "insert." A click sounded and a menu with more options dropped down. She slid the arrow to "files." A directory of file names blossomed on to the screen.

Leaning forward in her chair, she studied the names. She glanced at the paper on her desk that listed the confidential files she needed, files only accessible through secure computers in the office. One by one, she selected them. Small boxes representing copies of the files immediately appeared in the e-mail Jennifer prepared.

Closing the file directory, she rose from her seat and walked out of the cubicle into the darkness. She looked toward the windows that looked to the moonlit mountains. She listened for a moment. A fan from a heating unit rumbled in the distance. Nothing out of the ordinary.

Back in the cube, Jennifer opened her purse and pulled out a CD that she never let out of her possession. She knew never to leave it at the office. She put it on the tray in her desktop computer, reminding herself to make sure to remove it again when she finished. She waited while a program automatically started. She counted backward from 100 to make the time go faster. A moment later, a screen popped up asking for a password. In the low blue light, she keyed in an eight digit alphanumeric combination and clicked "OK" twice in succession. She sat back in her chair and waited.

The CD tray hummed as the computer read instructions from the disc. In less than a minute, a box appeared in the middle of the computer screen. "Encryption completed," it declared.

Jennifer clicked **send** on the e-mail with all the attachments. When the computer showed the package successfully transmitted, Jennifer opened her "sent items" folder and deleted her computer's copy of the e-mail.

She heard a loud clicking sound from across the building. She did not know if it was a person or creaking vents. She stood and peered over the cubicle looking for signs of movement. Quickly snapping her briefcase shut, she listened for further sounds, but only heard the whirring of the CD in its tray. She walked out of her cubicle, careful not to trip in the darkness, still listening for more noises. As she traveled further away from her cube, the whirring of the very sensitive CD she left behind grew fainter and finally stopped.

CHAPTER 5

Lokoma Village
October 27 - 3 am GMT

The croaking of frogs and cicadas faded. The muggy night grew silent. Hamara heard his breath passing slowly in and out of his nose. The musty smell of mold and decay mingled with the perfumed fragrance of new blossoms. Shifting his position on the smooth rock that acted as his seat, he listened to the first weak twitter of waking birds as the black of night paled to gray. Then, the first misty rays of morning sun passed through the narrow gaps in the thick jungle canopy, waking dozens of avian species whose songs sprang to life in a swelling cacophony.

He bounced a river pebble in his hand. The devil resided in this pebble – or so he was taught as a boy. Maboru, the magic in which he trained as both chief and diviner, taught that the pebble had great powers. It taught, for example, that a pebble could judge a man in a capital case. If it sank to the bottom of a bucket of water, it condemned the accused to a death sentence; if it floated, it freed him.

He could not imagine the dense pebble floating under any circumstances.

He wished that it did have magical powers. He would use it to make Sara well, to protect Jacob, to shield his village from sickness and violence. But if his experience as chief had taught him nothing else, it taught him that Maboru amounted to a centuries old scam. Somewhere along the way, people used it to gain favor with others, persuading the simple-minded of some magic to which only the diviner held the secret. Hamara now knew that magic amounted to nothing more than a mix of salesmanship, science and coincidence – and sometimes luck. The diviners, or witch doctors as whites once called them, played to the fears of uneducated, hardworking people who had never been more than a few miles from their birthplace. These people, their progeny and their ancestors lived in terror for centuries. First Islamic traders from the northeast and then local chieftains in league with the Europeans tracked them down, chaining and caging them like animals, ripping them away from everything they held dear.

With the healthiest and most attractive often the first to go, the tribes often experienced something akin to natural selection in reverse. Ultimately, their most beautiful young women found themselves among the many wives of the Islamic slave traders. The sturdiest women ended up chained inside the stinking holds of slave ships with the sturdiest young men; together they brought top dollar as laborers for distant plantations in the Americas.

The stories passed down to Hamara said that 30% of them died en route, disease rampant as they wallowed in one another's fluids and waste in the dark holds of the pitching ships.

Rolling the pebble between thumb and fingers, he scanned the trees and the red earth beneath them. How many times had his ancestors moved until they found this remote place? How far had they run from the sins of slavery? For five generations, the Lokoma tilled this very soil, mined its bauxite, conceived children on it and buried their dead in it. The magic of invisibility, not river pebbles or cowry shells, kept the Lokoma safe. The land and its location protected them. And they thrived through contentment with the blessings surrounding them in the rainforest. No promise of greater earthly riches tempted the Lokoma from their malaria-infested version of paradise.

Now white men had once more discovered them, just as they had in the time of the slave trade. Now, they came to bring a cure for malaria. But they also brought other, as yet unclear, agendas.

But mostly, Hamara ached that the alleged cure came four months too late for seven-year-old Ketta. That very real heartache doubled him over as he remembered holding her tiny body in his arms, again felt her warm breath on his neck; she whispered "Pa" before growing still. He did not let her go until the heat of her fever faded to cold, his own tears coating her cheeks as he gently laid her back on her mat.

Earlier this night, as he left the hut in the darkness, he softly touched Sara's forehead with the back of his hand. Sleep had again eased her fever. The Americans' magic vaccine would not get here soon enough for her. She would either pull through or not. Fr. Jim did not show up as promised. Adrian Guerra had come instead. Fr. Jim had never before let him down like that. Mariama said she dreamed that a spell made the malaria stronger than Sara's quinine tabs. Rumors had spread throughout the mountains that just such a spell had been cast over villages that refused to convert to the ways of Allah. Fr. Jim had assured her that the power of Jesus Christ would fight off any devil's spells, but he did not guarantee that the magic of Christ would make Sara well. It had not cured Ketta; her last Eucharist still digesting in her stomach when she expired. No, unlike the gods of the jungle and unlike the devils who falsely claimed to speak for Allah, Fr. Jim's God made no promises about miracles in this life.

That touch of honesty had caused Hamara to lead the Lokoma to conversion to the priest's religion. Hamara trusted Fr. Jim, relied on him. And Fr. Jim had brought Dave Clement and his family. They gave without taking because they were followers of the priest's God. Now Hamara prayed he had not been naïve about the American, that all of the generosity had not just been a long-term setup to use his people for personal gain.

He turned his hand palm down, the pebble dropping to the ground with an almost imperceptible thump. Falling to his knees, he made certain to face east. Bending forward, he prayed for the well-being of his family and of his people – and for time.

CHAPTER 6

Niwot, Colorado; Evan Conger's Memorial Service
October 28, 10:40 a.m. Mountain Time

Sheila Stratemeier pulled her overcoat tighter against the downslope winds that whipped over the eastern slope of Colorado's Rockies and across the St. Vrain Valley, charging up the hills over the village of Niwot. Atop one of those hills, she and nearly three hundred others stood on an undeveloped two-acre lot that had represented one of Evan Conger's fondest dreams. There, in the face of the chilling downslope bluster, underneath a roiling overcast sky, Sheila gathered with Evan Conger's friends and family to memorialize him this noon on the grassy crest of the hill. They stood in a large circle around a portrait of Evan draped in black and surrounded by fresh-cut flowers.

Evan's brother-in-law, a Lutheran pastor from Evan's hometown of Sioux City, Iowa, read Bible verses selected by Evan's wife, each meant to touch on some aspect of Evan that she sought to honor or simply remember this day. No choir sang. Sheila remembered that Michelle Conger knew her husband liked nothing better than the song of nature atop this hill facing the silver-white peaks of the Rockies. Here, she heard they planned to build their retirement home. The story that spread in the lab said that here, under the stars, often cuddled in a blanket with the top down on their red Thunderbird, Michelle and Evan listened to the hoot of owls, the songs of birds, and the howl of a coyote on a moonlit night. On some nights, the story went, great balls of tumbleweed bounced by them on the wind. Inevitably, Evan would break into a brief rendition of "Tumblin' Tumbleweeds," completely corny and entirely orthogonal to his public image. Sheila saw Michelle smile and wondered if she was thinking of it now.

"Evan led his life with complete regard for others," declared the pastor into a microphone to overcome the noise of the wind. "I knew him for over 35 years, since he first dated my sister, his wife. He championed DNA analysis as part of his research efforts at the Aldrich Institute. Someday, when the science matures a bit more, someone will study his DNA. It will show he did not have a single selfish gene. Here was a man who could have no enemies…"

Sheila shifted uneasily on her heels. She stared unconsciously at Claire McQuaid until Claire caught her looking. Sheila quickly looked away. In her peripheral vision, Sheila saw Claire's green eyes flash and her nose flare. A few people to her left, Sheila saw her one-time best friend Jennifer Winter, focused intently on the pastor's words. Always the dedicated follower, thought Sheila. For nearly a week now, since Conger's death, Jennifer had ignored Sheila's emails asking for help with Claire and Eldridge. Sheila did not know what form that help needed to take; she only knew that she could no longer handle it alone. And time was running out to de-rail this train.

Near the far corner of the podium, she recognized Dave Clement. It surprised her to see him without his wife. Mel inevitably accompanied Dave to events. Her absence presented an opportunity for Sheila to speak to him alone. Youssef Khalfani, the UN Secretary General, stood beside Dave. Occasionally, Khalfani and Dave exchanged whispered comments. The two men belonged to a small circle that centered around Evan in the quest to conquer tropical disease. With Conger gone, she needed to get to Dave. He could help her. And he needed to know what she knew about his daughter.

In her brief comments, Michelle Conger said that her husband had passed through just like the wind, but, just like the wind, he would keep coming back, ever churning in their hearts. She said that if and when they did find his body, it would not be him because, through the grace of an almighty and loving God, he had already come home.

"Feel the wind," she said. "Feel his presence. He is here with us now as he will always be."

Sheila wondered if she could be as hopeful as Michelle if it been her life partner taken in some inexplicable random selection. She prayed that Evan could actually be there. She prayed that his soul might intervene with God to bring her help. Urgently.

When Conger's service ended, the mourners lined up to hug Michelle and her two grown children. Sheila approached Dave Clement as he broke from the line.

"Hi, Dave." She touched the shoulder of his blue cashmere overcoat.

Dave turned. "Sheila. Hello."

"We need to talk. Alone."

"Sure."

Her eyes scanned the people nearby. She started walking, steering him away from the crowd. The wind would cover their conversation for anyone not right on top of them.

"Sorry we couldn't meet this morning," she said, leaning up to his face on her toes, her words barely discernible in the howling wind.

He leaned down toward her. "I understand. We'll reset."

"I don't know when," she said, "Security's getting tighter. They're watching me."

Dave leaned closer, struggling to hear her. "Who?" he asked. "Who's watching you?"

"The IRA thugs." She nodded in the direction of several men in large black overcoats.

"Can you send details to the cloud?"

Sheila held her Denver Broncos stocking cap on with one hand as it threatened to blow off. "That's just the point. I went in last night and found my access blocked. The Aldrich has blacklisted the cloud URL."

Dave's eyes widened. "So they must know. Can you use another one?"

She leaned close to his ear. "Won't make any difference. They know what to look for now."

"Will you be all right?"

"I'll be fine. But you need to know about Liv. Everything's not what it seems - "

A hand landed on Sheila's shoulder. She turned to see Mike Farley, the Aldrich head of security. She shook him off and turned back to Dave. She pulled out a business card from her coat pocket.

"Claire's ready to go," Farley said. "She and Mr. Clement have a lunch scheduled."

"I just wanted to introduce myself to our most important partner," Sheila said, handing Dave the card.

"I need another minute here," Dave said.

"Ten seconds, sir," Farley said, an Irish brogue apparent in a trilled 'r'. Then he stood there, hands folded in front of him.

"Alone," Dave said.

Farley looked back and forth at the two and then at his watch. "We need to go now," he said. He tugged at Dave's arm. Dave pulled back.

"It's okay, Dave," Sheila said. "We can talk again. Can't keep Claire waiting."

The security chief escorted Dave to McQuaid's limo. Dave looked back at Sheila. She nodded assurance.

"What did she want?" Farley asked as he squeezed Dave's arm a little too tightly.

"An introduction."

"Anything else?" he asked.

"You didn't give her time for anything else."

"Wait here," Farley said as he reached the back door of the limo. He leaned in and spoke inaudibly to McQuaid. He stepped back and Dave slid into the backseat.

From the back of the limo, Claire watched her security chief corral Dave. She did not want to add Sheila as a variable in managing the Prodeus exec. His relationships and ability to pull off the malaria project mattered more than ever with Evan gone.

"Strange place to network," she said to him as he entered the limo. As she spoke, she watched the retreating Sheila through the car's tinted window.

"I don't understand," Dave said.

"She's a good scientist, but we think she's getting a little claustrophobic in the mountain lab. Might be looking to make a change."

"Claire, I'd never pilfer one of your people -"

"I know that. Unfortunately, others might, and we can't afford to lose her."

"Pretty critical skills?"

"That. And she knows too many of our secrets."

He nodded.

Claire looked down at her carefully manicured nails. Physical perfection had been beyond her reach for years. Mourning a death reassured her that the physical mattered little. Her nails reminded her that she could pull it off for a little while. Uninvited, fire flashed into her mind. Shouts and screams.

"Can you imagine the horror?" Claire asked. "A lot of them died from smoke inhalation. A blessing, I suppose. Passing out. But many of them burned alive. Wide awake when the flames reached them..." Her hands trembled. "My God, Dave. Where do you run in a slowly burning airplane? The engine, the shell just kept flying while the plastic inside melted."

He reached out his hand. She gently waved him off and then dabbed a tissue under each eye, careful not to smear her make-up.

"I don't think Michelle really wants to find his body," she said. "Or what's left of it." She leaned forward and opened the limo's refrigerator. "Want a drink?"

"No," Dave answered. "No, thank you."

She found diet tonic water. Carbonation hissed as she pulled back the tab. "So, Evan's misfortune has left us a mess to sort out with W-H-O," she said as she moved the can to her lips.

Boulder, Colorado; Boulder Café
October 28 - 11:45 a.m. Mountain Time

In the face of blowing snow, Claire latched on to Dave's arm as her three-inch heels gingerly navigated the irregular cobblestones of the Pearl Street Mall. On the short walk from the curb to the granite entryway of the Boulder Cafe, wind whipped down the cavernous outdoor mall cutting through them like a thousand tiny icicles. Dave hunched forward into the frigid blast, regretting that he left his overcoat in the limo.

They entered the restaurant, stomping snow off their feet on a large red mat. The hostess, an anorexic-looking young woman with a small silver ball on the tip of her tongue and countless earrings, recognized Claire immediately.

"Good afternoon, Ms. McQuaid. We have your table ready."

They followed the hostess to a distant corner booth with high padded wooden backs suitable for privacy. Scooting across the bench to the window, Dave felt a twenty degree drop in temperature at the sill where nearly two inches of snow had already piled up on the outside ledge.

"Your trip home's going to be treacherous," Claire said. "Why don't you keep the limo after I'm dropped? It has chains. I'll have your car driven up when the roads clear."

"Thanks. I might. Let's see how bad this gets."

A waitress appeared with coffee. Dave continued the conversation they started in the limo. "Do you want me to handle Geneva on my own? Or do you want to join me?"

"No way. I don't know how to deal with those bureaucrats. Partnering's your strong suit." Claire poured a small amount of milk into her coffee. She scrutinized the cup for a few seconds before looking back to Dave. "Is your single status going to affect your focus?"

"I'm not single."

"But you're not living at home."

"It's... a hiccup. The love of my life is at home in Fort Collins. We'll fix things."

"Distracting, though."

"Emotionally, yes. But God spared me to dive deeper into the work. We're doing a very good thing and it needs my full attention."

"That's what happened? God spared you?"

"How else do you explain the odds of getting pulled out of the security line for a hand check for the first time in ten years? If that doesn't happen, I'm on that plane with Evan."

"That's true. God or not, someone was definitely looking out for you."

"I believe it was God."

"Who knows?" she said. "Some things are best kept a mystery."

"Maybe so."

"Anyway, I'm happy you have a guardian angel whether from God or not," she continued. "We're at a critical juncture. The partnership absolutely needs you. And we need you one hundred percent focused."

"Trust me. Coordinating the bureaucracy with the World Health Organization has my full attention. There's a lot to it without Evan's help. I'm a little concerned about taking my eye off the ball at the office, but I'll figure it out."

"Jennifer's good back-up. That's why I let you have her."

"The engineering team fights her."

"Little boys with toys don't like women driving the train."

"Unfortunately, there's some truth to that."

"You've always seemed immune to that kind of sexism, Dave. Makes you more endearing than you should be." She smiled as she opened her menu.

Dave looked at the menu but did not see it. He thought of Sheila's words. Something was in the works that could cure Liv. But Sheila's backdoor cloud communication channel to him was gone. Claire very likely knew what Sheila wanted to tell him. And probably knew about their communications. She would not tell him she knew because that would be admitting to spying on them. Now, it could be weeks before Sheila got back to him. He needed to find a way to get Claire to help, to tell him what Sheila wanted to tell him.

"So what else is on your plate?" he asked.

"Aside from the getting the firmware integrated with your product, we have a few other surprises in the works."

"Like a cure for AIDS?"

She peered over her menu. "Somebody tell you that?"

"Just makes sense."

"A cure for AIDS is incredibly ambitious. No one has even come close to a real solution."

"The kind of mountain you like to climb, isn't it, Claire? Who would have thought a malaria vaccine was do-able a few years ago? AIDS is a natural next step on the roadmap."

She put the menu down. "Officially, we don't have such a program. If we did, it would be strictly company confidential."

"We have a non-disclosure agreement."

"Specific to the PDNA project. Doesn't cover anything else."

"So let's expand the non-disclosure to cover it."

"There's nothing to disclose."

The waitress returned. Claire ordered the Moroccan salad and Dave selected a bowl of white chicken chili.

"There's a reason I asked," he said after the waitress left. "I thought you might make an exception to help me out."

"With AIDS?"

"You said you don't want me distracted. Well, I'm distracted."

"It's not business?"

"We could make it business."

"What is it?"

He hesitated briefly. "It's personal. But I need your promise that it stays between us."

"Sure." She leaned slightly forward, her eyebrows knitted.

"I need to find a cure or at least something that does a better job of holding it back," he said.

"AIDS?"

"Yes. It's still HIV, but it's the same issue."

Her eyes widened. "Is that why Mel threw you out? You have it?"

"No. Not me."

"Mel?"

"It's tougher than even that."

Claire sat back, her jaw dropping slightly. "Dear God, Dave."

"She's on her second drug regimen. She developed resistance to the first one and it looks like it might be happening again."

"That's concerning. You may want to look into experimental treatments. Expensive, but you should have plenty after the Prodeus public offering."

"I know that. And I'll do my part to make it happen. But I need your help in finding new drugs. Now. Not later."

She pondered him. "Maybe downstream. There's nothing right now."

"So you're working on something?"

She looked at him. She sipped her coffee. She looked out the window. "The snow's not letting up. You'll need the limo."

"Just tell me there's some kind of hope."

She turned back to face him. "I'll bet you've read everything written about the science in this, Dave. What do you think?"

Dave's grip tightened on his coffee mug. "Treatable," he answered. "Not curable."

McQuaid nodded. "That's the way I see it, too."

"But treatment's almost impossible with drug resistance," Dave said, choking down anger, mostly at himself for letting Claire in on Liv's secret in exchange for nothing.

"Almost," she said grimly.

"So can you help?"

"No."

Dave stared at Claire. She stared back. Finally, he looked outside, gazing at the snowflakes melting slowly on the window.

CHAPTER 7

Peggy's Cove, Nova Scotia
October 28 - 4:05 p.m. Atlantic Time

Seagull cries echoed along the shore. East across the cove that opened into Margaret's Bay and then the Atlantic Ocean, signs of impending nightfall appeared as the lowest layer of the horizon began to darken.

Marie raced along the rocky beach, her tiny, pink bare feet finding the soft sand in between the rocks. When she paused to catch her breath, her feet sunk into wet, black sand at the tide's ebb. It smelled and looked dirty here, like a gas station. Her mother told her it was from the plane. She could still see the search boats bobbing in and out of view in the distant waters of the inlet. The skinny ten-year-old remained fascinated by the sheer number of boats deployed. Mom's small coffee shop in the parlor on the first floor of their old Victorian home had buzzed every morning for over a week. Most of the people had been very nice and Marie had been careful with her manners.

Fr. LaBonte had been over often. Marie liked that. Fr. LaBonte was very kind to her and her mother. They needed him around this week, especially when the crying started. Marie did not like the crying. It made her cry, too. They talked about identifying the bodies. Marie did not want to know about the bodies. She watched a boat unload some in town a few days earlier. Someone unzipped one of the black body bags to show some official. It was all white, blue, and swollen, not really like a person at all. A black hole peered out of one of its eye sockets. Marie vomited on the planks outside the drug store.

Shaking her head to make the memories go away, the ten-year-old ran twenty yards down the beach to an untouched spot where the sand glistened white in the late afternoon sun. Springing from both feet, she splashed into the icy water, squealing with delight. Suddenly concerned, she stopped long enough to glance back at the house and make sure her unauthorized escape remained undiscovered. Her father would "blister her backside" if he caught her. Not seeing her parents or big brother, she began leaping over the small waves as they licked the shore.

"Ouch!" the ten year old shouted as her foot came down on something hard in what should have been soft sand.

Eighteen inches below the foaming surf, the edge of a gray rock peeked out of the sand. Marie bent down for a closer look. She hesitated to touch it as its image quivered mirage-like from the gentle wave action. The ache pulsing in her bruised foot intensified and she angrily reached down and yanked the rock from its repose.

She turned to throw it at the cluster of boulders she had navigated just a few moments earlier. The slick surface pressing against her fingertips caused her to pause in mid-wind-up.

She held a small black plastic box, not a rock at all. Padding over to a large flat boulder, she sat down to examine her find. Brushing away sand and small pieces of shell, she ran her hands over it. She turned the box upside down and sideways. finding several small buttons molded into the hard plastic. She pressed the one on top and nothing happened. She shook the box and held it against her ear. She heard nothing. She pressed the big button in front. A picture of a battery with a narrow bright red section appeared on the front of the box. Below the image, it said "5% charged." Marie realized she had found a phone.

She ran her fingers around the screen. The battery image went away, replaced by a box that said: "Low battery warning. 5% of battery remaining." She tapped the button below the message that said "Dismiss." Words appeared on the screen, but Marie had a hard time making them out in the reflection from the sun setting over her shoulder. She scooched around the rock, putting the sunset in front of her.

As if by magic, the black outline of the words blossomed and intensified before her, their edges becoming crisp and the print bold.

"Smoke's let up. They must have been able to open the cockpit windows. We're flying awfully close to the ocean. Have to wonder if this is sabotage. If it is, my team may be the target. Pilot just announced we're landing in Halifax. I can see the runway lights. Seems I've written this for myself. Better safe than sorry..."

Marie paused her reading as she hissed a frightened breath through clenched teeth. The image of the bloated body flashed back through her mind.

A new message popped up on the screen, blocking the other content.

Low Battery
Less Than 5% of Battery Remaining

Again she tapped the "dismiss" button below the warning and it went away.

"... Bad news. We flew past the airfield. Pilots couldn't keep us straight. Looked like the right wing would smash into the runway. We pulled up at the last second. Smoke pouring from under the cockpit door. As bad as before. Starting to come from the cabin vents now, too. The pilots cannot possibly see up there. As long as the electrical systems hold up, we have a shot. If I don't make it - if you find this -- please take this to some authority outside the United States' sphere of influence..."

Marie had no idea what a sphere of influence was.

"US authorities cannot be entrusted with this. The contents of the files on this phone may be the only hope to stop a horrible atrocity. If they have killed us, then our files will have been destroyed or archived where no one..."

Low Battery
Less Than 5% of Battery Remaining

She tapped the Dismiss button again.

"...no one will find them. If this phone survives us, please... The lights have just gone out. The electrical system. We need you now, God. It's this or prayers. This is my prayer. It can save others. Many, many others. There's fire now. The floor in back just erupted. Hot. People screaming..."

Very Low Battery - Please Connect to Power

She remembered the people crying at the coffee shop. As tears filled her eyes, she again tapped the Dismiss button.

"... Please take seriously. Take to someone who can be trusted..."

Fr. LaBonte, thought Marie.

"Look inside, you'll underst... "

The image of a battery with a red end on it appeared again on the screen. A new warning message appeared below it:

Please Connect to Power

Then the screen went black. Marie tapped around it. Nothing. The battery was dead.

Pondering the blank screen, Marie relived the images of the past several days, the body bags, the vacant bloodshot eyes of bereaved families, the empty eye socket.

She ran back to the house, hugging the box to her chest. She would take it to Father LaBonte. As the rear screen door squeaked behind her and slammed, her father called to her.

"Marie! Marie, is that you?"

She froze at the kitchen sink.

"Marie!" her father repeated.

She could hear his heavy footsteps clomping toward the kitchen. "Yes, papa, it's me," she called back.

"Where have you been?" His voice grew louder as he walked down the old hardwood in the hallway.

Marie scrambled to shove the phone into the back of the kitchen drawer where they kept the plastic bags. She had just finished shutting the drawer when her father entered the room.

"I was playing outside."

Her father looked down at the sand on her still bare feet. "Were you at the beach? What have I told you about the beach?"

He approached her, his arm cocked back across his chest, ready to backhand her. He smelled like beer. He always smelled like beer.

"No, sir, I wasn't," she said quickly, her hands now raised in front of her, poised to protect her face and head.

He looked again at her feet. The sand looked dry. There was plenty of sand in the yard. "You know better, right?"

"Yes, sir."

Her father studied her for a moment longer. He dropped his threatening arm to his side. "It's getting late. You need to stay in for the night. It'll be bedtime soon. I don't want mama finding you up when she finishes at the shop."

He turned and walked toward the living room where the TV played a re-run of "NCIS."

Relieved, Marie thought about retrieving the phone from the drawer, but she did not want to risk getting caught. She ran upstairs to her room. There, she thought about all the people on the plane, about how she would not be able to help now. Her father could never know she disobeyed.

She curled up on the bed, still in her clothes. Folding her hands in front of her lips, she felt her own warm, wet breath on them as she mumbled prayers for the victims and their families.

"…and dear God, please don't let that man's family see his eye. And please, please forgive me for not turning in the phone."

A few minutes later, she had cried herself to sleep.

CHAPTER 8

Lokoma village
October 29, 2:35 pm GMT

Hamara Karanja squatted beside Sara. She lay sweating profusely on a sleep mat spread on the hard dirt floor. Light crept through the thatch overhead, streaking Sara's five-year-old frame with splotches of brightness. His sinewed hand stroked her hair and temples. Her skin felt soft, smooth and frighteningly hot to his touch.

"Papa," she whispered, her wide eyes gazing at his silhouette in the dim hut, "I don't want to be sick anymore."

He reached for a clear, plastic bottle of warm water beside him. "Drink this, Sara," he encouraged as he placed the spout to her lips.

"Nooo," she moaned.

"Dear, you need to. We have to keep water in you or you could get sicker."

"Papa, I don't think I can get sicker."

"It will help make you better."

Conceding, she pursed her lips to receive the water and Hamara tilted the bottle slightly to allow the water to dribble over her lips and tongue. He had sent Jacob for ice at the community room earlier and he wondered why he was not back yet.

"How's that?" he asked his daughter.

"I think I have to go to the bathroom again."

"Are you sure?"

In the dimness, he could see her shake her head affirmatively. He put an arm under her shoulder and helped her up. The amulet strung around her neck caught on the mat. He disdainfully yanked it free; Mariama had insisted on it. She argued that, at worst, it would do no harm. Many of the Lokoma thought the cowry shell amulet could draw the fever out of a body.

Sara tried to wobble to her feet, but Hamara put another arm under her knees and lifted her into the air. He carried her out the door of the hut, leaning forward over her, trying to cast the shadow of his head and shoulders on her. In this way, he hoped to protect her eyes from the bright sunlight.

He walked ten yards to the common latrine. The stench always peaked at this time of day, the heat bringing the odors to life. He carried her inside and set her down on the small wooden commode. As soon as she settled, she let out a small howl. He heard the gushing of her bowels pouring into the stagnant water below. He steeled himself against the smell and kept a gentle hand on her shoulder as she shivered from weakness and fever.

Her little body had grown gaunt, her cheekbones and jaw over-pronounced as the fat stores and water that once puffed her face had now diminished to dangerously low levels. Through eye sockets deepened by this depletion, enormous brown eyes, glistening with tears, looked up at Hamara. She inhaled a deep swallow of the stale air and squeezed out a grateful smile as her head bobbed weakly on her small, frail neck. Her face creased again into pain. She tucked her chin into her chest and bent forward as more drained into the pit.

The quinine tablets Guerra brought had already run out. No more were available. Perhaps it was not malaria because Sara had never really responded adequately to the short treatment regimen. Damn this jungle, Hamara cursed to himself as he thought of all the disease that filled it.

He had asked how western medicine might treat her differently. In an elders meeting, one of the elders said he understood that western hospitals hooked people to intravenous lines and filled their veins with medicine to manage the disease. Hamara had asked how they could do the same. He received only blank looks, then a comment that it was impossible.

"We have no way to do this, Pa," Musa said, using the term of respect reserved for chiefs and diviners. "The fluids would have to be both sterile and refrigerated. And we would need the intravenous equipment. None of that is even available."

"What about Freetown?" the chief had asked.

"Certainly they would have this equipment at the hospital there," offered another elder.

"Where is the priest now?" challenged Musa.

Hamara looked upon his lifelong friend as though he saw a stranger. "Dead, Musa. Kidnapped and executed. You know that."

"She been shot by a witch, Pa," Musa persisted. "Maboru is needed. A traditional healing. The priest is in the afterlife with our ancestors, and they must be fightin' over your betrayal."

Hamara leaned in close to Musa and spoke softly. "That nonsense defies science."

"Science defies generations of learning by our ancestors. The ancestors remain around us watching, protecting us from the devils that fill the forest. Trying to bring us back to who we once were"

"And who were we?"

"A proud, ancient tribe with spirits that kept us well -- as long as we remained faithful to our ancestors."

"They did not save Ketta."

The elders grew silent. Musa studied his calloused hands for a moment, and then spoke. "All of us understand the anguish of losing a child. Every one of us has been touched by this scourge as either parent or sibling. It's not something we can understand. Perhaps, Pa, the spirit world needed her. Perhaps she even left to watch over us."

Hamara had no answer, thinking only that he wanted to feel her in his arms again, wanted to squeeze her close and find a way to keep her safe.

So now he stood in the pit latrine watching another daughter quivering with fever and deteriorating. They had to go to Freetown. He could not allow her to continue to suffer. He could not risk losing her. The rebel threat caused him to hesitate, but the others could manage without him for a few days.

After Hamara re-situated Sara on the sleep mat, Jacob arrived with ice. "The icemaker was almost empty again. I had to wait for more to be made."

Exhausted, Sara nodded off to sleep after a few minutes. Hamara met with his wife Mariama and Jacob outside.

"We need to get her to Freetown," he said.

"Finally," said Mariama with relief.

"Jacob, we could use your help," Hamara said.

Jacob pulled nervously at the pleats of his dark green shorts. "What about the rebels? What if we need to fight?"

"The bandits have moved southwest of here," Hamara said firmly. He did not think of the roving bands as rebels since the ceasefire; he viewed them as pure criminals out for plunder. "They have no reason to come back this way. Even if that happens, we'll be back long before they could re-deploy to this area."

"What if you're wrong?"

Hamara had entertained the same question, but he knew he needed to show confidence, as both father and village chief. "I'm not wrong. And if I were, the last thing any of us should do is try to fight the automatic weapons of these bandits with our machetes and arrows. The elders know to run. We can rebuild again. These huts are not worth the lives of our children. We'll get the land back; they can't destroy that."

Jacob thought for a moment. "What about my mother?"

"I spoke with her. She wants to stay here with your grandparents."

"But I thought she wanted to leave."

"No, Jacob, she's not ready for that."

"I'm staying with her."

"I need you, son."

Jacob's dark eyes narrowed, blood rushing to his face. "So does my mother. Your first wife."

He turned and walked off rapidly, fists clenched, shoulders hunched forward and his little boy legs churning.

Public Offerings continues in
Public Offerings Book Two:
The Price of a Life

You can buy each of the four books in the Public Offerings series at your favorite book store in either eBook or print format.

Or you can purchase all four books and get the complete Public Offerings series in a single volume at your favorite bookstore, including the Amazon Kindle bookstore at http://goo.gl/MdkLFY

Public Offerings Book 1:   Birthright

Public Offerings Book 2:   The Price of a Life

Public Offerings Book 3:   Killer Priest

Public Offerings Book 4:   Children on the Altar

Public Offerings Complete: All Four Books in One

Learn more: www.PublicOfferings.net

Follow: www.Facebook.com/PublicOfferings

APPENDIX

ABOUT THE AUTHOR

With *Public Offerings*, Bob LiVolsi won the Writers League of Texas prestigious manuscript contest for best thriller. Bob was also a finalist in the same competition for best narrative non-fiction. He started his career as a journalist and was managing editor of the Daily Kent Stater at Kent State University. There, he won the Sears Congressional Internship for his investigative coverage of racial tension on campus.

A former high tech executive on teams that took two companies public, Bob applied his experiences in the mercenary world of high-stakes investment to Public Offerings. As a vice president with Hewlett Packard and in his roles in building new companies, he traveled the world, partnering with large corporations, governments and other international organizations. Bob has also consulted for VRI, a vaccine research start-up. His private support of missions in sub-Saharan Africa and Central America brought him closer to the day-to-day challenges presented by disease, poverty and tyranny. In the mid-1990s, he began online communication with a missionary priest in Sierra Leone where he learned about the horrors there not yet reported in the western press. The priest disappeared and was assumed killed. He became the inspiration for Fr. Jim Reilly in *Public Offerings*.

Bob LiVolsi lives in Austin, Texas, with his wife and two daughters. He is currently writing *Courtship of Innocence*, the sequel to the *Public Offerings* series.

CHARACTER SUMMARIES

Clement Family, Fort Collins, Colorado

Dave Clement

> Dave is the father of Liv Clement and husband of Mel Clement. As VP of Operations and Business Development at Prodeus, he is the main driver of partnerships to deploy the Portable DNA Analyzer (PDNA) with malaria vaccine pilot in West Africa. Dave is the likely successor to Ed Hepp as CEO of Prodeus. Claire McQuaid, Executive Director of Aldrich, relies on Dave's partnership and his relationships in the pharmaceutical industry and with international aid organizations

Liv Clement

> Fifteen year old daughter of Dave and Mel Clement. Liv is a good student and volleyball player at Ft. Collins High School where she is a sophomore. She is on anti-retrovirals to manage HIV. She insists to her parents and doctors that she has participated in no risky behaviors that would lead to HIV. She has not had a blood transfusion, another possible source of HIV. She keeps her HIV very secret; her friends, teachers, and coaches do not know she has it. She frequently writes in a diary to help her cope

Mel Clement

> Liv's mother and wife of Dave Clement. Mel works as a mortgage broker, but now seldom goes into the office, working from home to be present for Liv. Mel is frustrated with Dave for constantly prioritizing work over family and feels he is not doing enough to help find answers for Liv's HIV.

Aldrich Institute, Colorado

Claire McQuaid

> Executive Director of the Boulder, Colorado-based Aldrich Institute. She has spearheaded the development of the malaria vaccine to be tested in Sierra Leone with the Lokoma tribe and others. Claire's body is disfigured from wounds incurred when she was young. She is passionate about her work and feels a duty to change the world on a grand scale. She helped put Ed Hepp and Prodeus in business where she sits on the board. She plans to have Dave Clement replace Ed as CEO when Ed's Parkinson's Disease advances to the point where he cannot carry the CEO workload. Importantly, Claire relies on Dave to smooth the way for cooperation with locals in Sierra Leone and with significant allies such as Evan Conger at the World Health Organization (WHO).

Sheila Stratemeier

> Lead developer for the malaria vaccine at the Aldrich Institute. Sheila works out of the Aldrich's secretive mountain lab in northern Colorado's Rawah Wilderness, high up in the mountains near the Medicine Bow Range. Sheila is troubled by the alternatives that Claire and the Aldrich are considering for deployment of the malaria vaccine; Sheila and Jennifer Winter, who works for Dave Clement at Prodeus, are close friends going back to the days when they were protégés at the Aldrich Institute fresh out of grad school.

Eldridge Perry

> Director of Drug Discovery for the Aldrich Institute. Eldridge works out of the firm's mountain lab in Colorado's Rawah Wilderness. Sheila Stratemeier and Jennifer Winter both reported directly to Eldridge when they worked there together; he is still Sheila's manager today. A very secretive and mysterious man, Eldridge compartmentalizes work assignments among his researchers and developers so that no single one of them has a complete picture of the company's plans and strategy.

Lokoma Village, Sierra Leone

Fr. Jim Reilly

Irish missionary priest who serves the people of Sierra Leone. Fr. Jim feels a special fealty to Chief Hamara Karanja and the Lokoma tribe. He baptized Chief Karanja and the tribe members when they converted from a local tribal religion three years ago. He is itinerant, traveling from village to village and often saying Mass outdoors. Dave Clement and Fr. Jim have been friends since Fr. Jim gave a fundraising sermon at Dave's church in Colorado eight years ago. Since then, Dave and Mel have contributed funds and time to help the Lokoma through hard economic times during the civil war in Sierra Leone.

Hamara Karanja

Paramount chief of the Lokoma nation in the northwest mountains of Sierra Leone. Hamara considers Dave Clement a friend through Dave's efforts to bring medical missions to the Lokoma, bringing items such as eyeglasses and prescription medicines. Hamara is married to Mariama Karanja who has given birth to two daughters: Ketta and Sara. Ketta died recently at age seven from malaria. Sara is five and her family dotes on her, particularly since the loss of Ketta. Hamara's oldest child Jacob, age 10, is his son by his first wife, Ani. Hamara was married to both Ani and Mariama simultaneously, but had to choose one when he converted to Catholicism, as polygamy is outlawed by Church law. He chose Mariama. Jacob holds this against his father.

Jacob Karanja

Hamara's oldest child, Jacob was born to Hamara's estranged wife Ani. Age 10, he lives with Ani, his birth mother, in the chief's compound along with Ani's parents, Mariama and his sister Sara. Jacob aspires to be a chief like his father and seeks ways to demonstrate his manhood, but he is troubled that his father threw out his birth mother.

International Aid Organizations (NGOs)

Adrian Guerra

> The West African Country Director for the World Bank, Adrian is based in Freetown, Sierra Leone. Adrian persuades Dave Clement to place the malaria vaccine pilot in Sierra Leone, not strife-torn Nigeria. Adrian wants Chief Karanja to sell the Lokoma tribe's ancestral land to another tribe, ostensibly to get the Lokoma to more reliable medical care and safer environs in Freetown away from the criminal bands that still wander the bush, years after the official end of the civil war. Chief Karanja opposes such a move, believing he owes it to his tribe and to their ancestors to keep the Lokoma where they are. Adrian has to sign off on the World Bank funds needed to subsidize the malaria vaccine project in Sierra Leone.

Evan Conger

> Director of sub-Saharan tropical diseases for the World Health Organization (WHO), Evan is a reliable and experienced hand in health care administration and drug discovery. He served as Executive Director of the Aldrich Institute until the President of the United States tapped him to be Surgeon General. After serving in the administration, he could not go back to the Aldrich where Claire McQuaid was doing an effective job as his replacement. Instead, he took the job at WHO, hoping to make a difference there, particularly with regard to malaria. He started the malaria vaccine research at the Aldrich and is working with Dave Clement to bring the pilot project for the vaccine to Sierra Leone. WHO's endorsement of the effort will be critical to its deployment and its financial success. Evan and Dave have known each other for years and have a close, trusting relationship. Evan is the kind of man everyone looks up to as a mentor.

Public Offerings continues in

Public Offerings Book Two:

The Price of a Life

You can buy each of the four books in the Public Offerings series at your favorite book store in either eBook or print format.

Or you can purchase all four books and get the complete Public Offerings series in a single volume at your favorite bookstore, including the Amazon Kindle bookstore at http://goo.gl/MdkLFY

Public Offerings Book One: Birthright

Public Offerings Book Two: The Price of a Life

Public Offerings Book Three: Killer Priest

Public Offerings Book Four: Children on the Altar

Public Offerings Complete: All Four Books in One Volume

Learn more: www.PublicOfferings.net

Follow: www.Facebook.com/PublicOfferings